Young Pilgrim's Progress

For David and Eva

Young Pilgrim's Progress

Chris Wright

Lighthouse
eBooks

Young Pilgrim's Progress

Chris Wright

Text and line illustrations copyright
© Chris Wright 2007

Cover illustration copyright
© Malcolm Bourne and Mark Orriss 2007

Published by
Lighthouse Christian Publishing
SAN 257-4330
5531 Dufferin Drive
Savage, Minnesota, 55378
United States of America

www.lighthouseebooks.com
www.lighthousechristianpublishing.com

INTRODUCTION

THIS INTRODUCTION tells you how this book came to be written. If you want to skip it and get straight on with the story, that's fine. You can always come back to this page later – or not at all. To tell you the truth, I'm not too keen on long Introductions myself!

In the year 1677, an Englishman was in prison in Bedford, England. His crime? He had been preaching without a license, and his name was John Bunyan. Only ministers from the Church of England were allowed to hold services of worship in those days, and the punishment for breaking the rules was severe.

John Bunyan says he had a dream in which he saw people traveling through life as though they were on a map. One man found the way to the Celestial City. John Bunyan decided to write the dream as a story. He called the man he had seen in his dream – the man who found the way – Christian. He called his book *The Pilgrim's Progress*.

Over a hundred years ago, Helen L Taylor realized that children found *The Pilgrim's Progress* hard to read and understand. Much of Bunyan's book consists of deep discussions between Christian and the people he meets. So Helen Taylor rewrote the first part of *The Pilgrim's Progress* in

1889 and the second part in 1891, using children as the main characters. She called the first part *Little Christian's Pilgrimage*, and the second part *Christiana*.

Thirty years ago, I found an 1889 copy of *Little Christian's Pilgrimage* in a secondhand bookshop. My children and I thought it was one of the best books we had ever read. It was certainly better than any simplified version of *The Pilgrim's Progress* for children I had seen, so then I bought the 1891 edition of *Christiana*. I went through the two Victorian books and changed some of the wording to suit older readers. In 1982 Bridge-Logos published the story in two separate volumes: *Young Christian's Pilgrimage* and *Christiana's Journey*.

But young people today are not only different from the readers in John Bunyan's time, they are different from the original readers of Helen Taylor's Victorian story, and different again from the readers of my 1982 version. Although Helen Taylor's book has recently been reprinted in its original form, many of today's readers will consider much of the language and events rather childish. We read a lot about "the poor little boy" in her book, and how "he sobs". And Helen Taylor misses revealing Bunyan's identity of Goodwill at the Wicket Gate, which I think is a shame.

I feel that the time has come for a brand new edition of *The Pilgrim's Progress* that is suitable for readers who are older than those Helen Taylor probably had in mind – indeed, for people of any age who want a simplified version of Bunyan's story but don't want a childish account. I have nothing but praise for Helen Taylor, and without her hard work you would not be reading this book now. However, she was writing for young readers in the nineteenth, not the twenty-first century.

I am letting the main characters tell the story in their own words, while bringing many of John Bunyan's characters and events back to life. Mrs. Bats-Eyes is one example (yes, she really is one of Bunyan's people), but Christiana's baby sister Innocence is not in Bunyan's original. Helen Taylor probably invented Innocence to make her book appeal to tiny children. Now Innocence has gone, and Samuel has reappeared in his rightful place as the second oldest brother. This makes the story stronger for the readers I have in mind. To anyone who thinks what happens to Faithful in Vanity Fair is too gruesome to repeat here, bear in mind that far more people face death for their faith today than they did in John Bunyan's time.

In spite of making changes to both John Bunyan's and Helen Taylor's words – both long out of copyright – I have tried to keep the old-fashioned atmosphere intact by moving much closer to John Bunyan's book. I hope you enjoy reading this story as much as I have enjoyed writing it.

Chris Wright
Bristol, England

PART 1

CHRISTIAN'S JOURNEY

CHAPTER 1
The City of Destruction

I SAT ALONE on the hill above the city. It had been a long day. My friends had gone home some time ago, leaving me to think about the heavy weight on my back. I knew I'd feel better as soon as I could find a way to get rid of it.

I looked at the gloomy streets spread out below. Even with the sun shining, everything seemed broken and neglected. The city would only look worse when the winter winds and rain came.

The City of Destruction. No wonder I felt unhappy in a place with a name like that. There were days when I'd do anything to get away. The only good times, for me, were when the visitors came with their messages of hope.

"Leave this city now, Christian," they said. "Go, while you're young and strong, and travel to the Celestial City where the King lives. You'll be safe there."

Whenever I asked my friends if they would go with me, they told me the Celestial City was only a make-believe place. No place could be better or safer than our city, they said.

Part 1 - Christian's Journey

Now, on the hill, I felt sure the visitors were speaking the truth. A few months earlier I had found a special Book, and in it I read exactly the same things the visitors were telling me about the King and the Way to him – and how the City of Destruction would be destroyed one day.

I showed the Book to two of my friends, but all they did was laugh. "That Book was written a long time ago. It's no use to anyone now," one of them said. "The King's army hasn't come, and we don't think it ever will. So take it easy, Christian. Let's enjoy ourselves while we can."

So there I sat, looking down at the grimy city, wondering if I'd be able to find the Way to the King on my own. The more I thought about it, the more I was afraid I'd get lost if I tried. Even so, I had to get away. Opening my Book again, I read about the King's own Son who had once come here to the City of Destruction, and invited everyone to go to live with him.

I noticed how dirty my clothes had become. I was nearly fourteen, so I'd worn them a long time, and they were frayed and shabby. The more I tried to live a good life, the worse they looked. "Even if I *do* find the Celestial City," I decided, "I can't expect the King to receive me dressed in nothing but rags."

My mother was already living with the King in his City, and of course she wanted my father and me to join her there. When I got home, the woman who came in every day to look after me asked if I was ill. "Christian, you look so miserable," she said. "Are you running a fever?"

I told her I wanted to go to the Celestial City, and she laughed exactly as my friends had done.

"Just get that nonsense out of your head," she snapped irritably. "There *is* no Celestial City, my lad, and if you go wandering along the roads after those visitors you'll soon get lost."

So I went to bed without saying anything more. But it was a long time before I could get to sleep.

Part 1 - Christian's Journey

CHAPTER 2
Evangelist

When I went out the next morning, the sun was shining brightly again. Some of my friends asked me to join them, but I told them, "I can't. I've made up my mind to go to the Celestial City. Will you come with me and help me find the way?"

"You're crazy," they said. "You keep going on about that stupid Celestial City. Why don't you just go there – instead of talking about it and spoiling our fun?"

I didn't feel like arguing, so I let them walk off to do whatever they were planning. Presently my friend Christiana came down the street. She stopped to speak to me, which made me feel a little better. Christiana was the sort of friend who understands when things aren't going well.

"Why do you listen to the visitors, if they make you unhappy?" she asked, which is something I'd been wondering myself. Then without waiting for an answer, she said, "Come on, let's climb the hill."

Although Christiana said she didn't believe the stories in my Book, she never laughed at me. I think, in a way, she wanted to believe they were true – perhaps she even thought they were.

"You know," I said, as we walked up the path, "I *have* to go to the King. I've not told you before, but I've got a burden to carry. The King is the only one who can take it from me."

"Burden?" Christiana asked, sounding surprised. "I can't see a burden."

"It's on my back, and it feels so heavy it makes me tired."

Christiana came round behind me, looking puzzled. "You must be ill, Christian, if you think there's something on your back."

"I'm not ill," I insisted. "Just because *you* can't see it, doesn't mean it's not there."

We reached to the top of the hill, and were so out of breath that I forgot about my plans for my journey, and it wasn't until I got back that night that I began to think again of the Celestial City.

The house was empty. The woman who looked after me had gone home, and my father wasn't back from his work – as usual. He had an important job in the city, and always came home late.

The next morning I went round to Christiana's house, hoping to go out with her again and persuade her to travel with me. Her parents had both gone to live with the King, and she told me she had too much to do at home, as she was now like a mother to her four brothers. My other friends said they wanted nothing to do with me, so I wandered into the meadows outside the city wall, and sat down on a grass bank to read my Book.

The more I read, the more convinced I became that I needed to find the King. As I read about the King's Son, tears came my eyes as I thought he might not want anything to do with me – even if I found him.

After a while I heard someone coming, and looking up saw one of the visitors on his way to the city. His name was Evangelist. I'd seen him before, and I think he recognized me because he came over. I looked the other way. My eyes were red, and I felt foolish.

"Why are you upset?" Evangelist asked.

He could obviously see I'd been crying, and I found his voice was comforting. So I told him how I wanted to get away, and how my friends made fun of me, and how no one seemed to believe there really was a place called the Celestial City.

"And what is the Book in your hand?" Evangelist asked.

I showed it to him. "This is why I'm crying," I said. "My Book tells me there's no hope for me if I stay in the City of Destruction. Is the Book true?"

"The Book is true," Evangelist said quietly. "But haven't you read the good news in there as well?"

I put the Book down. "What good news?" I asked.

"Your Book says the King loves everyone. He even loves you, Christian. If you start your journey, he'll watch over you all the way. Then, when you reach the Celestial City, you'll be safe for ever."

"I've read that," I agreed, "but I still don't know what to do. I'd start now – if I could find the Way."

Evangelist turned and looked across the fields, along the path by which he'd come. "Do you see a high wall in the far distance?" He pointed with his finger.

But my eyes were still cloudy with tears, and I wasn't able to see anything clearly.

"Look," Evangelist said, "there's a light shining above it. Can you see that?"

I thought I could, so I nodded.

"That light marks the start of the Way to the Celestial City. When you get to the wall you will see a large door. No one can open that door, but there is a small door in the large one, called a Wicket Gate. You have to go through it to begin your journey."

"Is that the only way?" I asked.

"Indeed, yes, there is no other way. The King's Son made that Wicket Gate. Now, I will show you a promise to all travelers."

Evangelist opened my Book and pointed to some words spoken by the King's Son. I read them aloud. "I am the way and the truth and the life. No one comes to the Father except through me."

Evangelist smiled as I looked up at him in surprise. "Now, Christian, if you want to meet the King, you must go quickly to the Wicket Gate – and make sure you knock."

Part 1 - Christian's Journey

CHAPTER 3
Obstinate and Pliable

I noticed a group of my friends creeping closer while Evangelist was speaking to me. I wondered why they were taking such an interest now. This must be the first time they'd ever bothered to listen to the visitors.

I told Evangelist I couldn't wait to get started, and he waved me on my way. As I began to run across the fields towards the light, I heard my friends call out, "Where are you going, Christian?"

I didn't say anything, but just kept running.

"Running away, running away," they chanted. "Christian is running away!"

"Come back," I heard one of them shout. "You'll get lost."

I blocked my ears with my fingers, and kept running. There was no way now I was going to let anyone talk me out of going.

I unblocked my ears when I thought I was far enough away, and was surprised to hear the voices of two of the boys, Obstinate and Pliable. They were older than me, but the three of us often joined in games together. Obstinate wasn't a pleasant companion, for he always wanted his own way, and Pliable used to give in for the sake of peace. I didn't care much for either of them, but I liked Pliable better. Difficult, and Easily Led. How well their names suited them.

"Come back, Christian," Obstinate called. "You're stupid if you believe there's a Celestial City."

"Wait for us," Pliable added. "We're coming with you."

I heard them shouting but refused to wait, or even look round again.

"If they take me back," I kept thinking, "I may never have another chance to get away."

So I ran as fast as I could, but I soon began to feel tired because of the weight on my back. Even if no one else could see it, I knew it was there.

Obstinate and Pliable were taller and stronger than me, so it didn't take them long to catch up. "Where exactly do you think you're going?" Obstinate demanded, grabbing hold of my shoulder. "What do you mean by making us run after you?"

"I'm going to the King's City," I said, shaking myself free. "Are you coming with me?" I didn't think they were, but I could call their bluff.

Obstinate laughed. "Why would we do that? Destruction is a wonderful city, and there's so much to do here. I'm happy enough with my friends."

I shook my head. "We'd all be a great deal happier with the King. I've told you before, our city is a dangerous place."

"As if *you* know anything about it," Obstinate said. "Why do you keep talking such nonsense?"

I felt I had to defend myself. "It's not nonsense. It's written in my Book."

This made Obstinate laugh again. "How many times do I have to tell you – your Book is full of rubbish! There's not one word of it true. Now, are you coming back or not?"

Obstinate sounded angry, and I could feel my heart begin to beat faster and faster, but I wanted to sound confident. "No, I'm not going back. I'm going to the King."

"Go on, then," Obstinate said. "Come on, Pliable, we could have saved ourselves the trouble of running after this crazy boy. He doesn't know when he's well off."

But Pliable stood still. "Don't laugh at him," he said. "Just supposing the Book *is* true. Christian will be better off than we are. I'm going with him."

"Yes, please come with me," I said. And I meant it. I was going to need some help along on the Way. "You don't know how happy we'll be when we're living with the King."

"Are you *sure* you can find the City?" Pliable asked. He obviously still had doubts.

I nodded. "Evangelist told me what to do. We have to go to that light in the distance, and a man at the Wicket Gate will let us through."

"You don't really mean to say you're going?" Obstinate jeered. "Why, even if there *is* a Celestial City, you two will never find it."

Pliable moved to stand by my side, which made me feel glad. "I may as well go as far as the Wicket Gate, and see what the road is like," he muttered.

"I'm not surprised at Christian," Obstinate continued, "but you, Pliable, you ought to have more sense. Just come back with me, and I'll not tell anyone about it."

For once Pliable seemed pleased to be having his own way, and he said, "It's no use talking, Obstinate. I've made up my mind. So I'll say goodbye, if you won't come with us."

"No, thank you. I'm glad to get rid of you both." With a mocking smile, Obstinate turned back towards the City of Destruction.

Part 1 - Christian's Journey

CHAPTER 4
The Slough of Despond

"Now," Pliable said, when Obstinate had left us alone, "tell me what sort of place this Celestial City is."

"It's wonderful," I replied, as though I knew all about it. Well, Evangelist said is was good there. "Haven't you heard what the visitors say? It's where the King and his Son live, and his people never feel unwell or unhappy. They wear shining clothes that can never fade, and no one ever grows old."

For a moment, Pliable looked excited. Then his face fell. "If it's as good as that, I don't suppose they'll let *us* in."

"Evangelist told me the King has promised to let *anyone* in who asks."

"Well, he didn't tell *me* that."

"You didn't meet Evangelist." Pliable had a point, but he seemed to be missing what Evangelist had said several times about the Way being open to everyone. "It says the same thing in my Book, so don't worry about it. I'm sure the King will be pleased to see you."

"Well, tell me something else. What will you do when you get to the City?"

"First of all I'd like to see the King, and then I'll look for my mother. She went there three years ago." One of the visitors had told me she was with the King and his Son in the Celestial City, and that's what I told Pliable.

Pliable seemed to have nothing but questions. "How long will it take us to get there? Did you ask Evangelist? We might go a little faster, I think."

"I wish I could," I said, feeling tired already. "It's this burden on my back that's causing the problem. At times I can hardly walk."

Pliable was just saying, "What do you mean by pretending you have a burden to carry?" when suddenly his feet began to sink into the ground. "Help!" he cried. "What's happening?"

I was sinking faster than Pliable, into a large bog of soft mud. "We have to get out," I said, which was rather obvious to anyone.

But we felt frightened and confused. The wet ground started to suck us down, like dangerous quicksand. I remembered too late that we were passing the Slough of Despond, and it was definitely a dangerous place. Every move we made seemed to pull us further into danger. We were already up to our waists in oozy mud.

"See what a mess we're in," Pliable shouted. "And it's all *your* fault, Christian. I wish I'd never come. If it's like this now, what's the rest of the journey going to like? If I can ever get out

Part 1 - Christian's Journey

of this swamp, I'm going straight home. You can go on by yourself if you like!"

I didn't answer. My clothes were covered with dark sludge, and I was convinced that at any moment I was going to be sucked under and drowned. I desperately wished Evangelist would come to help, but I couldn't see anyone – apart from Pliable – and he was no use at all. Far away, across the fields, the light shone above the Gate to the Way of the King, and behind me lay the City of Destruction. I was stuck between the two, and sinking deeper and deeper.

Pliable turned away from the light, and somehow managed to drag himself out of the bog. When I looked back, I saw him running home as fast as he could go. At that moment I decided perhaps Evangelist was wrong, and the King didn't want people like me traveling along the road to his City.

"I'm so stupid," I thought. "I can't even get safely across these fields. What would happen to me if I came to a high mountain or a deep river?" And once more I struggled to find firm ground.

Then, when I had almost given up, I heard a voice calling, "Wait, I'm coming to help you."

CHAPTER 5
Help

I looked round when I heard the voice. "Who are you?" I asked.

"I'm called Help," a young man said. "I'm one of the King's servants. I saw you struggling in the Slough. How did you fall in?"

Even though I was still sinking, I told Help what had happened. "Evangelist said I was to go to the Wicket Gate, and I forgot about this bog."

"Didn't you see the stepping-stones?"

"No, I was talking to Pliable and we weren't looking at the ground,"

"Where is Pliable?"

"He got out, but he didn't try to help me." My voice must have made it sound like an accusation. Well, I was angry with Pliable, that's for sure. "And you'd better do something quickly, because I'm being sucked deeper every time I move."

"I'll have you out of there in a minute." Help smiled confidently. "I was wondering why the King sent me over the

Part 1 - Christian's Journey

fields today, but I can see it was because he knew you'd need me."

I put out my arm, and Help caught hold of it firmly and began to pull. As soon as I came free from the sticky mud, I stood on the edge of the marsh trembling with fright, hardly believing I was safe.

"Thanks," I said, which was a bit of an understatement. "I could never have got out by myself."

"No," Help told me, "I don't think you could."

"So why doesn't the King make a good path round it?" I asked.

"The King has always tried to make the way easier by filling the Slough with good things, but people keep throwing their rubbish in, so the mud spreads out onto the path. In any case, you saw what happened with Pliable. He wasn't prepared to keep going when things became difficult. In a way, the Slough is a test to see who really wants to find the King."

"Well," I said, "I really do want to go to the Celestial City."

The Celestial City. I knew I'd not done marvelously so far. Maybe Pliable had made the right decision in running back to the City of Destruction. "If the Way is going to be like this, perhaps I'd better wait until I'm older," I said.

Help shook his head. "No, don't wait. People a lot younger than you have started their journey at the Wicket Gate. The King will watch over you, and if you call out to him he'll send somebody to help you whenever you're in trouble."

"Are you sure?" I asked. "All my friends say I'm stupid."

Help smiled. "Never mind what people say. When you're one of the King's pilgrims, you'll be safe." He was kneeling on the ground as he spoke, wiping the mud from my clothes with tufts of grass.

"I've made a mess of them," I said, "and they weren't much good before I fell in."

Help got up, laughing. "Don't worry about your clothes. You'll be given new ones before you reach the Celestial City. Keep your eyes fixed on the light over the Wicket Gate, and walk there as quickly as you can. And if you meet anyone, don't let them talk you out of going."

"Just tell me one thing," I said, as Help got ready to leave. "Have you ever been to the City?"

"No, but I've been to its Gates. Then the King gave me some work to do for him, and I can't live in the City until it's finished."

It didn't seem to me that my journey would be over in a few days. Perhaps it would take a lifetime. "How long will it take me to get there?"

"I can't tell you that. For some people the journey is long, and for others it's short. But the King will let you into the City at the right time. Now I must go. If you're frightened again, call to the King and he'll hear you."

I thanked Help, but now I'd lost sight of the light above the Gate. "Please tell me the way again," I called as he walked away.

"Follow the path across the fields. Do you see that mountain? It's called Mount Law. Don't go anywhere near it," Help said. "There's a village called Respectability on the other side of it, and you need to keep well away from that place too. The people who live there call themselves the King's servants. They pretend to love and obey him, but they don't care about anything but their own pleasure."

I seemed to remember hearing about these people. "Did they once live in the City of Destruction?"

Help nodded. "They were afraid to stay there because of what the visitors told them. But they decided it was too much trouble to go to the King's country, so they've built houses and made fields and gardens for themselves. And now they think they're safe because they live such good lives."

Something told me they were wrong.

CHAPTER 6
Young Worldly-Wiseman

As I made my way towards the light above the Wicket Gate, I met a boy coming across the fields. He was a bit older than me, but I recognized him as young Worldly-Wiseman, who often came to the City of Destruction to visit his friends. He'd boast that he knew everything there was to know about living a good life. I wanted to avoid him, but Worldly-Wiseman across forward to meet me.

"Hello, Christian," he said in a surprised voice, "are you coming to visit us?"

I shook my head. "I'm going to the Wicket Gate."

"The Wicket Gate? Whatever for?"

"To get rid of my burden."

Worldly-Wiseman put a comforting arm on my shoulder. "I understand all about those burdens," he said, with an encouraging smile. "It isn't everybody who can feel them, but when you can, there's no comfort until it's gone."

I was surprised to hear Worldly-Wiseman speak in this way, for my all friends in the City of Destruction told me my

Part 1 - Christian's Journey

burden was in my imagination. "I hope I'll not have to carry it much longer," I told him. "I need to get to the Wicket Gate."

"Whoever put it into your head to go there?" Worldly-Wiseman asked in surprise. "And why are you covered in mud?"

I decided to tell everything exactly as it had happened. "I met a man called Evangelist, and he told me to go through the Wicket Gate. But on the way I . . ." I bit my lip in shame. "I fell into the Slough."

Worldly-Wiseman smiled. "Evangelist? Yes, I've heard of him. He may be kind, but he's a bit . . . You know . . ." He tapped his head. "Look here, Christian, I can tell you a much better way to lose your burden, and you certainly don't need to go on a long journey – or fall into any more marshes. I can imagine what Evangelist said. He tells everyone the same thing."

"But I trust him," I said, leaping to Evangelist's defense. "I didn't listen to him when he first came to the city, but as soon as I starting reading my Book I knew he was telling the truth."

"Trust him?" Worldly-Wiseman sneered. "Look what's happened to you already. You've been in that horrid Slough, and if you go through the Wicket Gate, you'll find worse troubles than that. There are giants, lions, dragons, wild beasts and all sorts of dangers, and more than likely you'll die of hunger along the way. So why would anyone want to travel on *that* road?"

"But my burden is so heavy," I sighed, hardly listening to what young Worldly-Wiseman was saying. "Evangelist told me there's only one way to get rid of it, and that's to go through the Wicket Gate."

"You can't even see the Gate from here," Worldly-Wiseman said, laughing. I realized he was even worse at making fun of me than my friends in the City of Destruction.

"I have to look for the light over it," I told him.

"I can't see any light," Worldly-Wiseman said. "Can you?"

I had to admit I couldn't. "Not from here," I said.

Worldly-Wiseman laughed again. "I'm telling you for your own good, Christian. You might as well stop all this nonsense and listen to me. Do you have any family?"

"My father works in the city, and my mother's in the Celestial City."

Worldly-Wiseman shook his head and stopped laughing. "There isn't any Celestial City, and there's no King. Don't start thinking you'll see your mother again. She's gone. For ever."

I felt a little panic run through me. Supposing Worldly-Wiseman was right? Not only had the Wicket Gate gone, there was no longer any sign of the light. So maybe the whole idea of the Celestial City was make-believe after all.

"Well, you can do as you like," Worldly-Wiseman told me, "but I think you're just silly. How did you ever know you had a burden?"

"Everyone has a burden. I read about it in the King's Book."

"I thought so. That Book is all very well for clever people, but people like us can't understand it. You read it, but you've no idea what it means, so you just get your head full of nonsense. Now, I'll tell you what to do. Don't go back to your city, because you'll always feel frightened there, and it really isn't a nice place to live."

"I've no intention of going back," I said, for I already knew it wasn't a nice place. I'd been living there all my life.

"If I were you, I'd go over Mount Law and call at my village," Worldly-Wiseman advised. "If you can climb the mountain without coming to harm, you can go down to the village of Respectability where I have some friends. If you tell them I sent you, they'll give you somewhere to stay and treat you well. Then in a few days you'll forget all about your burden, and I don't suppose you'll ever feel it again."

Worldly-Wiseman spoke so confidently that I was starting to believe what he said. It would certainly be nice to live near my old home, and see Christiana and my other friends sometimes.

"You can't do better than to take my advice," young Worldly-Wiseman continued. "Never mind about Evangelist and Help, and don't bother looking for the Wicket Gate. Just climb Mount Law, and go to the village of Respectability. Call at the first house you come to."

He put his hands in his pockets and walked off, whistling to himself. To my shame, I forgot all about the King and his message, and set off to climb the mountain.

CHAPTER 7
Evangelist Again

I went on towards Mount Law as quickly as I could, but my burden seemed to grow heavier every minute, until at last I was ready to fall down under its weight. Walking was almost impossible, and I wondered whether I'd ever be able to get over the mountain to the house where Worldly-Wiseman's friends lived.

But when I turned the corner of the footpath that led over Mount Law, I almost forgot my burden, for I'd never before seen anything so scary. The side of the mountain was steep, with rocks that looked ready to fall onto the path.

I went a little way, but I was soon too frightened to take another step. I fancied I could see lightning, and flames of fire darting out between the rocks, and I have to admit that I shook all over with fear.

"Oh, I wish I hadn't come," I cried out. "What am I going to do?"

Just then I saw a man hurrying down the path. As he came nearer I could see it was Evangelist. He had no smile on his face this time, and I felt so ashamed and miserable that I almost wished the rocks *would* fall.

"What are you doing here?" Evangelist asked.

I hung my head down.

"Aren't you the lad I spoke to outside the City of Destruction?"

"Yes," I said quietly. There was no point in pretending I was someone else.

"Didn't I show you the way to the Wicket Gate?"

"Yes."

"Then why are you here, trying to climb Mount Law? This isn't the way. No one has ever managed to climb this mountain without having a serious accident."

"I didn't mean to do wrong," I said, "but I met someone I knew. He said I could get rid of my burden in the village of Respectability on the other side. But now I'm sure the rocks are going to fall on me, and I'm scared."

Evangelist shook his head. "Listen to me, Christian. The King sent me to tell you about the Celestial City, and you had his promise that he will love you and watch over you."

"He hasn't taken care of me at all," I said. "What's the King done to help me?"

"He's been calling you to go to him," Evangelist said. "When you were in the City of Destruction he showed you through your Book that he wants you. When you fell into the Slough of Despond, he sent Help to pull you out. You've read in your Book that the King will always take care of those who trust in him. So why did you believe what Worldly-Wiseman said, and start climbing Mount Law?"

Of course, that made me feel even more ashamed. "Worldly-Wiseman told me he knew an easier way for me to get rid of my burden," I mumbled in embarrassment.

Evangelist laid his hand gently on my head. "You have grieved the King," he told me, "but if you're sorry, he'll forgive you."

"I'll never disobey him again," I promised, and I really meant it. The sight of those rocks and the lightning was like a nightmare. "But are you *sure* the King will forgive me, even if I don't climb Mount Law?"

Evangelist seemed less stern now, and he even smiled. "Yes, the King will always forgive you. Believe me, Christian, no one has ever been able to climb Mount Law. That is why the King's Son made a Way that starts at the Wicket Gate."

"And can I still go through it, or will the man who guards it turn me away and send me home again?"

"Oh, Christian, you still don't understand. The King's Son doesn't turn anyone away. You have only to knock, and the Gate will be opened for you. Keep close to me, and I'll lead you safely away from this mountain."

It felt good to be walking with Evangelist, and be led back into the fields. Mount Law with its terrible overhanging rocks was soon left behind, and I could once again see the light above the Wicket Gate.

Part 1 - Christian's Journey

"If you hurry," Evangelist told me, "you'll reach the Wicket Gate before dark. You can stay there and rest until the morning."

Then with a smile he said goodbye, and I started once more on my journey – in the right direction this time.

Chris Wright

CHAPTER 8
The Wicket Gate

I walked quickly, for I certainly had no wish to be out in the fields after dark. By this time I felt so tired that it was a great relief to see the Gate, just as the sun was setting.

It was exactly as Evangelist had described it: a small door let into a massive one, in a high wall. The large door, that Evangelist said could never be opened, stood in a beautiful stone archway, and over it hung the lamp that was burning so brightly that I'd been able to see it from my city, even when the sun was shining. Round the top of the arch I noticed some words carved into the stone. I looked up at them.

KNOCK, AND THE DOOR WILL BE OPENED TO YOU

"That's what Evangelist told me," I said to myself.

I could see a small hammer hanging by the Wicket Gate, so I used it to knock gently. I listened, but couldn't hear anyone coming, so I lifted the hammer higher and knocked harder, again and again. Then the Wicket Gate was opened by someone who had the kindest face I'd ever seen. It's impossible to describe my feelings.

He smiled. "Who are you?"

I could sense the man already knew my name. Knew all about me. "My name is Christian. Who are you?"

"I am Goodwill. Are you from the City of Destruction?"

"I am." In spite of these questions, I felt sure Goodwill was going to let me in. "I want to go to the King," I added.

Goodwill opened the Wicket Gate wide, and took me by the arm. As I was stepping in, he gave me a sudden pull on my arm.

"Why did you do that?" I asked in surprise.

Goodwill looked serious. "The evil prince has built a castle near this Gate. Sometimes, when he sees anyone entering my Gate, he orders his soldiers to shoot arrows at them, to try to hurt them before they can enter."

I looked out and saw several arrows lying on the ground, and was relieved when Goodwill closed the Gate firmly behind me.

"Now I'm safe," I thought, and hoped I was.

Goodwill led me into the house, and made me sit down to rest while he prepared some food.

"Who told you how to get here?" Goodwill called from the kitchen.

"Evangelist," I answered, "and he said you'll tell me the Way to the Celestial City."

"Yes, I'll tell you. But why are you alone? Have you not brought any friends or family with you??"

"My mother is already with the King," I said. "And my father has so much to do at work that he can't spare the time. My friends only laugh at me and call me stupid. So I've come by myself."

"Did no one want to go with you?"

"Two friends called Obstinate and Pliable ran after me," I explained, "but Obstinate was angry. Pliable said he'd like to go with me, but we fell into the Slough of Despond and he was frightened. So he went back to the City of Destruction. I thought I'd never get out, but Help came just in time."

"And what then?"

I felt my face turn red, for I was as bad as Pliable. I also had a strong feeling that Goodwill knew exactly what had happened to me, but I still wanted to tell him about it. "When I met young Worldly-Wiseman I listened to him," I explained. "That's why I went towards his village called Respectability. The road is dreadful, and I was afraid the rocks on Mount Law were going to fall on me."

"That mountain has been the end of many people who have tried to find the Celestial City," Goodwill said. "Sadly, there are people still trying to reach the City that way, but if they make even the smallest of mistakes on their climb, they never reach the top. And so far, no one has managed it. Why did you make your mind up not to climb?"

"I was already starting up the mountain when Evangelist found me," I explained. "He showed me the proper way here, and told me never to try climbing Mount Law again."

Goodwill smiled. "Well, you've entered my Gate, and that means you're one of my pilgrims. Tonight you must sleep here, and tomorrow I'll show you the Way to the Celestial City where my Father lives."

CHAPTER 9
Interpreter

When morning came, I felt rested and ready for another day's journey. Goodwill took me outside and showed me a narrow pathway that seemed to go in a straight line across the open countryside. There was a wall on one side, which made it even easier to keep to the path.

"Are there any turnings?" I asked. "Only I won't know what to do if I come to a place where there are two roads."

"The Way of the King is always straight," Goodwill told me, "and any paths leading out of it are crooked."

"But is the right path always obvious?" I was afraid of going wrong again.

"Well," Goodwill said, "the wrong paths are usually wide, while the right path is the narrow one. If you look carefully, you'll not mistake it. But don't walk too close to the wall. It marks the boundary of the evil prince's land."

I wanted to get rid of my burden as soon as possible. "Do you think you could help me off with it?" I asked, pointing to

Part 1 - Christian's Journey

my back. "I'll be able to walk much better without this great load."

"You must carry it until you come to a special place where it will fall off," Goodwill said, "and then you will never see it again. I want you to understand where your burden has gone, and why."

"I'll certainly be glad when it's gone," I said with a sigh. "Is the place far?"

"Not too far."

That didn't sound too close either. Somewhere along the Way I'd probably need to rest. "Will I pass any houses?"

"About the middle of the day you will come to a house that belongs to a man called Interpreter. Knock on his door and he will show you many wonderful things, and explain their meaning to you."

The morning seemed bright and pleasant, and I enjoyed my walk. Everything around me seemed new, and the air felt so fresh that it seemed to take away the weariness that had been with me since leaving the City of Destruction.

"Well, there's nothing to hurt me here," I told myself. "Young Worldly-Wiseman didn't speak the truth when he said I'd be frightened. That *mountain* was the frightening place."

The words that Goodwill spoke to me were running round in my mind. He had said entered *my Gate*, become *my pilgrim*? The man who had welcomed me into the Way *must* be the King's Son, and that was why the Wicket Gate was the only place to start. I remembered Evangelist showing me some words in my Book, spoken by the King's Son. *I am the Way and the Truth and the Life. No one comes to the Father except through me.* Oh, how I wished I'd taken more notice of Goodwill at the time!

Just when I was beginning to think I'd like to take a rest, I saw a large house near the road. I decided it must be the house of Interpreter, so I went up to the door and knocked. But no one came. I kept knocking until I heard the latch being drawn back. When the door opened, an elderly servant asked me what I wanted.

"I'm a pilgrim," I said, and I noticed a friendly smile on the servant's face. "I'm on my way to the Celestial City. I stayed with Goodwill last night, and he told me the owner of this house is his friend. May I speak to him?"

The servant went back and called his master, and soon Interpreter came out and put his hand on my shoulder. "What can I do for you?"

"I've been told you can show me some special things in your house, if I ask," I said. My voice sounded quiet, for I couldn't help thinking that although Interpreter would be pleased to have older pilgrims calling, young ones might be in the way. "Goodwill told me I could come to see you," I added, just to make sure there was no misunderstanding about why I was here.

Interpreter smiled. "I can see you're one of the King's pilgrims. Come in, and we'll find some things that you'll like to see."

Part 1 - Christian's Journey

He led me into the hall where the elderly servant was still waiting. Interpreter asked for a lamp, then he opened the door to a large room.

I couldn't believe what I was seeing. The house was such a smart building, almost like a palace. Yet here was a room that was thick with dust. Interpreter called for a man to come and sweep the floor. As soon as the man started using the broom, clouds of dust rose up and we all started to choke. Interpreter then called for the elderly servant.

The servant carried a huge jug of water, and splashed it over floor. Immediately the dust stopped rising and the dirt was washed away, leaving the room clean. I asked what was happening.

"The room is like our hearts," Interpreter explained. "There is no way we can clean them ourselves. The more we try, the more mess we make. The water is like the healing touch of the King's Son. He is the only one who can make our hearts clean."

It was only later that I began to understand the meaning of Interpreter's words. In the next room curtains covered the windows, but the light from Interpreter's lamp filled the whole room with a dazzling brightness. On the wall opposite the door was a picture, and when I saw it I stopped and stared.

It was the picture of a Shepherd who looked like Goodwill who kept the Wicket Gate. He was walking over a mountain path. All around him, amongst the rocks, were briars and thorns that had torn his clothing. His feet were bleeding where the rough stones had cut them. In his arms the Shepherd carried a sheep.

"Was the sheep lost?" I asked, although I suppose that was obvious from the picture.

"Yes," Interpreter told me, "lost and almost dead. Can you see how tired it looks, and how its fleece is torn and soiled? But the Shepherd heard its cry, and he never rested until he found it. Then he carried it home in his arms."

"It must have been a hard path," I said. "The stones have cut the Shepherd's feet."

"It was a hard path, but the Shepherd didn't mind that, because he loved that sheep."

"Who is he?" I asked. "Is he Goodwill?"

Interpreter held the lamp high so I could see the picture even more clearly. "The Good Shepherd is our King's own Son and, yes, he let you in at the Gate. Just as the Shepherd loves his flock, so the King's Son loves us. The pilgrims are like that sheep. You must always remember who is watching over you."

"*I'm* a pilgrim," I said suddenly, looking up at Interpreter. "I was lost, just like that sheep."

"A pilgrim, and a young sheep in the flock of the Good Shepherd. Now I'll take you to see something else."

Part 1 - Christian's Journey

CHAPTER 10
Passion and Patience

Interpreter took me upstairs to a room where two small boys were sitting, each in his own chair. One of them seemed quiet and happy, but the other was crying, looking cross and discontented.

"These two boys are staying here for a time," Interpreter said. "The one crying is called Passion, and his brother's name is Patience."

"What's the matter with Passion?" I asked.

"He's a foolish boy," Interpreter explained. "There are some beautiful gifts coming from the King, and the children are each to have their share. Patience is willing to wait, but Passion is upset because he can't enjoy everything now. He wants to have his pleasure today, instead of at the proper time."

Just then the door opened, and a man came in carrying some books and toys, and spread them on the table in front of Passion. The boy looked pleased, and wiping away his tears began to look at his treasures. Among them were some bags filled with gold coins. When Passion saw these he held them up in his hands, and laughed at Patience who had nothing.

"Passion is happy now," Interpreter said.

"Are the King's gifts *better* than these?" I asked in surprise.

"Far better. They are treasures that cannot be spoiled, and Patience is wise to wait for them."

"Passion's laughing now," I said, starting to understand what was happening, "but I imagine Patience will be happier in the end. Am I right?"

Interpreter nodded. "You must remember that everything I show you is meant to teach you something. I want you to learn that it's not wise to wish too eagerly for pleasant things, until the King sends them. Watch carefully."

As I watched, all Passion's treasures turned to dust, and his fine clothes turned to rags.

"You see," Interpreter said, "the King knows exactly what is good for each of us, and he will always give us what will make us really happy. If we behave like Passion and try to be happy in our own way, we are sure to be disappointed."

In another room we saw a fire burning brightly in the grate. An unpleasant-looking man kept throwing water onto the flames, but instead of water putting the fire out, it burnt even more brightly. I shielded my eyes against the heat and asked why the fire stayed burning.

Interpreter smiled. "You cannot see beyond the flames," he said. "If you could, you would see the King's Son pouring oil on the fire to make it burn more brightly. The man with the water is the King's enemy, but however hard he tries to extinguish the flames, he can never put them out. So it is with us. If the King's Son is in control of our lives, we need never fear what the enemy can do. Like the fire, we will always burn brightly for the King. Now, I have one more thing to show you, and then you must be on your way."

Interpreter took me out of the house, and we saw a beautiful palace. On its flat roof people were walking about, all clothed in gold.

"Is this one of the King's palaces?" I asked.

"Yes, but it's not easy for anyone to enter it."

Just inside the door a man sat at a table with a book in which he wrote the name of anyone who went into the palace. I could see a crowd of people outside. They looked as if they wanted to go in but were afraid. Then I noticed some soldiers in armor standing in the doorway, and the people who were outside were unwilling to go past them.

Presently a man wearing armor like a soldier came out from the crowd and went towards the table near the doorway. The man at the table wrote his name in the book, then the soldier put on his helmet and drew his sword and rushed at the soldiers. He fought with them for a long time, and although he received many wounds, he got into the palace at last. Then all the people on the palace roof started to shout and sing with joy.

I thought I could get the point of that picture too. "Does that mean we're not to be frightened, because the King will help us and take us safely into his City?"

"Yes," Interpreter told me. "I knew you'd understand it for yourself. It's getting late now. You must eat here and stay the night."

Part 1 - Christian's Journey

CHAPTER 11
The Cross

I don't think I slept very well that night. I was too excited to think that at long last I really was on my way to see the King.

After an early breakfast, Interpreter saw me on my way. Beyond the large house the Way of the King was still easy to find, for the high wall continued along the side of the road. "Be sure to keep to the straight path," Interpreter warned me, "and as long as you do that, you'll be safe. But remember, the high wall belongs to the land of the evil prince."

I had almost forgotten my burden while I was with Interpreter, but as I hurried along, and the morning began to grow hot, I felt its weight again and wished more than ever I could get rid of it.

"Goodwill told me I'd come to a place where it would fall away," I said to myself. "I hope it's not much further."

Presently I came to a small hill by the side of the road, with a Cross on the top. As I began to climb the path to look at it, just for a moment I imagined I could see the King's Son who had once hung on it, his hands and feet bleeding. As I looked, I felt the bands fastening my burden break. It fell from my shoulders and tumbled its way to the bottom of the hill. I turned to see what had become of it, but it had fallen into a deep pit and was out of sight.

At first I was so surprised I could scarcely believe that the man who had been on the Cross had caused me to lose the burden, for it had been such a trouble to me.

"I must be dreaming," I said to myself, but although I stood still for a few minutes, and rubbed my eyes, the burden didn't come back. The King's Son had taken the weight from my shoulders for ever. It was such a wonderful feeling. I knew I would never see that burden again. The King's Son would make sure of that.

"Now I can walk as quickly as I like," I said to myself, but although the Cross was empty, I stayed looking at it for a long time with my heart full of joy and thankfulness.

I remembered reading in my Book how the King's Son had once come to live in the City of Destruction, and in the towns and cities round about. Although he was loving and good, some of the people hated him. At last they seized him and put him to death by nailing him to a wooden cross. But death couldn't hold him, and he came alive again. This must be the Cross where the King's Son had been punished instead of me, so the King would no longer be angry. As I stood below the Cross, I could understand why Evangelist and the other visitors never grew tired of talking about him.

Part 1 - Christian's Journey

"Perhaps they all carried burdens like mine," I said aloud. "And when they came here to the Cross they lost them, just as I have done." As I looked up, tears came into my eyes.

Just then I heard voices behind me, saying, "We bring you peace."

I turned round quickly and saw three figures in robes that shone so brightly the light hurt my eyes, and I had to look away. "Christian, you have often displeased the King," the first one said, "but I have come to tell you that you are forgiven, and the wrong things you have done will not be remembered anymore."

I turned to look again, but the light still dazzled me.

Then the second figure said, "Christian, your clothes are torn and dirty. I wish my pilgrims to wear clothes that are clean, so I am giving you new ones."

Before I had time to think what to say, my shabby clothes were gone, and I found myself dressed in new clothes from the King.

Then the third figure set the mark of the King on my forehead, and gave me a roll of parchment with a seal on it. He called it a Roll of Faith with the Seal of Promise, and told me to read it and be sure to take care of it, for I would need to show it at the Gates of the Celestial City.

After this, the three went away, leaving me to rub my eyes and think about everything the King had done for me.

I gave three leaps for joy and started singing a song of joy. Surely I had just met the King's Son who took my burden, the King who gave me new clothes, and his Spirit who sealed me with the King's mark. I really was one of the King's own children!

Part 1 - Christian's Journey

CHAPTER 12
Simple, Sloth and Presumption

I never thought I could feel so happy. I realized I would have started this journey long ago if I'd known how good it was to be a pilgrim. Then I remembered Christiana, and thought what a pity it was that she'd not come with me. But I wondered how she could have managed it anyway, for she had four younger brothers to look after, because her parents were living with the King.

I was walking on with my mind full of these things, when I came across three boys a bit older than me. They were fast asleep by the side of the road, with their ankles bound together with chains. They must have been trapped by a servant of the evil Prince, and didn't even seem bothered.

The day was hot, and they probably left the path to lie down to rest for a while. I remembered Interpreter's warning, and knew I had to rouse them.

"Get up," I said urgently. "This isn't a safe place. Can't you see someone's fastened your ankles together?"

One of them spoke without even opening his eyes, "I don't see anything to worry about. My name is Simple. Let me have a minute's peace."

But I said, "I'm sure you're in great danger. Quick, let me help you to undo those chains."

The second boy sat up and began to rub his eyes. He looked at me. "My name is Sloth, so what's the use of disturbing me?" he said. "Just go away. We'll be coming later – when we've had a good rest."

The third boy said he was called Presumption. He tried to stand up, but because of the chains round his ankles he fell over. "Aren't we allowed to do as we like?" he complained, settling down again. "If we choose to sleep here it's our business, not yours. Get on with your own journey, and don't meddle with other people."

In a few minutes they were all sleeping as soundly as before. I turned away, feeling sorry that they wouldn't listen to me, or believe they were in the power of the evil prince.

At that moment I heard a noise, and saw two boys climbing over the wall. They dropped onto the Way of the King, and ran up to me.

"Where have you come from?" I asked in surprise.

The boys said their names were Formality and Hypocrisy. "We've been living in the land of Vainglory," Formality said. "And now we're starting our journey to the Celestial City to see the King."

"But don't you know you have to come in at the Wicket Gate?" I asked. It wasn't as though I was any sort of expert on this, but I remembered what Evangelist had told me.

"Oh," the boys said, "that Gate is much too far from our country. Everyone cuts across the fields and climbs over the wall."

The more I thought about it, the more certain I was that the King wouldn't want people to start their pilgrimage like this, so I said, "You're wrong. People can't do that."

"Oh, don't you bother about it," they said scornfully "Our people have been doing it for nearly two thousand years. Anyway, does it matter, as long as we're on the right road now? You came in by the Gate, and we came over the wall. Are you in any better place than we are?"

"I still don't think you should have done it," I said.

"That's nonsense," they told me. "We're just as good pilgrims as you are, except that you have such fine clothes – which likely somebody had to give you, because your own were like rags!"

These words hurt me, and I wanted to be rude back to them. But I'd read in my Book that the King's servants must speak gently, even when angry words are spoken to them.

So I waited a minute, then said quietly, "That's quite true. The King gave me these clothes because my own were indeed like rags. I'm glad he did, because when I get to the Celestial City he'll know I'm one of his pilgrims. And you may not have noticed it, but I have the mark of the King on my forehead, and

I have a Roll of Faith to read now and to show at the end of my journey. Do you have any of these?"

The boys laughed and shook their heads.

"That's because you didn't come in at the Gate," I said quietly.

But the boys only laughed again as they walked with me. Soon we came to the foot of a steep hill. A signpost said this was Hill Difficulty, and its finger pointed to a narrow track that ran straight up. *The Way of the King*, it said. I'd had enough of trying to climb mountains, and hesitated. I could see two smooth paths running around the hill, one on each side. One path was marked *Danger* and the other had a sign saying *Destruction*.

The Way of the King looked rocky and steep, but this time I knew I had to take it. A spring of cool water bubbled up in a pool by the wayside. As I felt thirsty, I paused for a refreshing drink before starting the difficult climb.

I looked back to see if Formality and Hypocrisy were following me, but they had already taken the other paths, one going to the right and the other to the left.

"What's the good of climbing up that steep place?" they called to me. "These two paths are much easier. They go round the hill, so we'll join up with the Way of the King again on the other side. We'll see you there."

I wondered how anyone could read the names of those paths, yet still go along them. Surely Formality and Hypocrisy must understand that the only safe path was the one going straight over the hill. Well, they would have known if they'd

Part 1 - Christian's Journey

only taken the trouble to obey the King and begin their pilgrimage in the right way. Formality and Hypocrisy, I thought. Show and Pretence. They were certainly able to put on a show of following the Way of the King when things were easy, and now they thought they were taking a shortcut round the hill.

As I climbed, I looked down to see what was happening to these two. Far from going safely, I could see Formality following his path into a dark forest that seemed to go on for ever. He was unlikely to find his way out, and would probably collapse with hunger and cold.

The path on the other side of the hill, the one Hypocrisy had chosen, looked no safer. It led between two steep cliffs. The last I saw of him, Hypocrisy had slipped and fallen onto some jagged rocks, where he lay without help.

CHAPTER 13
Hill Difficulty

The path up the hill was certainly a hard one. The rough stones and sharp pieces of rock that covered the ground hurt my feet. As it became steeper, the only way I could keep climbing was by going on my hands and knees. The sun shone fiercely, for it was already the middle of the day. As it beat down on my head, I felt hot and tired.

"I'm glad I didn't try to climb this hill yesterday," I said aloud. "I could never have carried my burden up here."

When I was halfway up the hill, the path became easier and I was able to walk again, and the stones didn't seem quite so sharp. Still, it was hard work climbing, and when I came to a small shelter I felt so glad. A notice said the shelter had been built by order of the King, so his pilgrims could have a place to rest.

I went in and sat down. It felt cool and quiet inside, and I thought I'd take the time to look at my Roll of Faith. I read it for a while, but instead of then making my way to the top of the

Part 1 - Christian's Journey

hill, I sat admiring my new clothes and thinking of many things, until my eyes closed and I fell asleep.

I didn't wake until the sky was already beginning to grow crimson with the sunset. I thought I heard a voice calling to me not to be lazy, so I jumped up and continued to climb the steep path.

Near the top of the hill I met two boys running down towards me. When they saw me, they stopped.

"What's the matter?" I asked. "You're running the wrong way."

"My name is Timorous," cried the larger of the two, shaking with fear. "We were going to the Celestial City, but the further we go, the more danger we find. So we're going home. This is my friend, Mistrust."

"Yes," Mistrust told me, "we've just seen two enormous lions lying on the path. We don't know if they're asleep or not, but I'm sure if we try to pass them they'll rip us to pieces."

This made me frightened, and I said, "What shall *I* do?"

"Why, come back with us, of course," Timorous said in surprise. "You can't be so foolish as to go anywhere *near* those great beasts."

"I don't know," I replied. "If I go back, I'll never see the King."

"Well, you certainly won't see him if you go on," Mistrust told me. "Those lions will kill you, that's for sure."

Would they? Evangelist and Goodwill and Interpreter had all told me that although I might often be frightened and in trouble, the King would help me and take care of me. "I'm not going back," I said. "The lions might be asleep. Come on, let's all go together and see."

"Not us," Timorous and Mistrust cried. "We're going home, and hope we can get there safely."

So they ran back down the hill, and left me to go on my way.

I couldn't help being worried, and I said to myself, "I'll look at my Roll of Faith, and see if there's anything in it about these lions."

But when I put my hand in my pocket the Roll wasn't there, and though I felt all through my clothes I couldn't find it anywhere.

I remembered how I'd been warned to take care of the Roll, for I would need to show it at the Gate of the Celestial City.

"I can't go on without it," I said aloud. "What can I do?"

I felt scared.

Part 1 - Christian's Journey

CHAPTER 14
The House Beautiful

I soon forgot about the lions, and could only think how careless I'd been in losing the most precious of the King's gifts. Then I remembered the small shelter where I'd spent the afternoon. Perhaps the Roll had fallen there. I had jumped up so quickly that maybe I'd not seen it fall.

"Oh, how could I be so foolish?" I cried, falling down on my knees and asking the King to forgive me. "I ought to have rested there only a little while, and I wasted so much time. Now it will be nighttime before I reach the top of the hill."

I turned round and went back, looking carefully everywhere along the path in case I'd dropped my Roll of Faith on the Way. At last I reached the shelter, and there on the floor, just under the bench where I'd been sitting, I saw my lost treasure.

Quickly I picked it up, thanking the King out loud for letting me find it. But going back for the Roll had delayed me, and although I climbed back up the steep path as quickly as I could, the sun had set before I reached the top.

"It's my own fault," I said aloud. "If I'd thought more about the King, and less about my new clothes, I would never have lost it. I'm sorry," I said, dropping to my knees again. "I was thinking about the gift and not the Giver."

Then I remembered the lions, and wondered how far I was from them. I knew that these savage beasts were likely to prowl about in search of prey during the darkness, and as the shadows grew deeper and deeper round me, I felt even more anxious.

Just before night came, I saw a large building in the distance. As I hurried along, I saw that it was a great house, and the Way of the King would lead me close to it. A cottage stood just inside the gates. I supposed this must be the caretaker's lodge, and I walked quickly, hoping I might be allowed to stay there for the night.

The path became more and more narrow, and when I'd almost reached the gates to the house I saw the two lions that had frightened Mistrust and Timorous. The great beasts stood just in front of me, one on each side of the path. There was only a small space between them, and I thought that if I tried to slip through it, they would be sure to attack me.

"Do not be frightened," the voice of a man called out suddenly. "The lions are chained. Keep in the middle of the path, and they cannot reach you."

I looked at the lodge, and saw that a man had come out of the door carrying a lantern. So I went on, even though I was afraid, taking care to keep in the middle of the path. At that moment I noticed chains glistening in the light from Watchful's

Part 1 - Christian's Journey

lamp, keeping the great creatures back. So although they roared as I walked between them, they were not able to stretch out their huge paws to touch me.

As soon as I'd passed the lions, I clapped my hands for joy and ran quickly towards man standing outside the lodge.

"Who are you?" I asked.

The man smiled. "My name is Watchful. I know pilgrims are often afraid of the lions, and cannot see the chains until they get close. I am glad you were brave enough to get past."

"I'm glad too. What's the name of this house?" I asked.

"It is called the House Beautiful," Watchful told me. "It belongs to the King. He built it as a place for his pilgrims to stay on their journey. Are you going to the Celestial City?"

I nodded, feeling much bolder now that the lions were behind me. I told Watchful how I'd left the City of Destruction and come through the Wicket Gate. "Last night I slept at the house of Interpreter," I said. "Can I stay here for the night?"

"It is already dark," Watchful said. "Why are you traveling so late?"

I told him how I'd dropped off to sleep on Hill Difficulty and lost my Roll of Faith, and how I'd gone back to look for it.

"Well," Watchful said, "I will call the young ladies of the house. As you are one of the King's pilgrims, I am sure they will be able to take care of you."

So we walked together to the door of the large house, and Watchful rang the bell.

CHAPTER 15
The Four Sisters

"There are four young sisters living in this house," Watchful said as we waited in the porch of the House Beautiful. "The oldest one is called Discretion. Here she is now."

"Why did you call me?" Discretion asked Watchful, then seeing me, she put out her hand and shook mine.

Watchful said, "This young pilgrim is on his way to the Celestial City, and it is too late for him to walk any further tonight. So he would be glad to stay here, if you are willing to take him in."

Then Discretion asked me many questions. She wanted to know where I'd come from, and why I'd left my home. She also asked me who had shown me how to get onto the Way of the King. I told her all that had happened on my journey.

"And what is your name?" she asked at last.

"Christian," I said, hoping I'd be allowed to stay. "I'm tired and I really would like to sleep here tonight."

"Yes, of course," Discretion said, with a smile. "I'll call my sisters."

She went back into the house and brought them out. Two looked quite a bit older than me. Their names were Piety and Prudence. Charity, the youngest, was about my age.

"This is one of the King's pilgrims," Discretion said. "I think we can make room for him in the house, can we not?"

"Oh, yes," Prudence said.

"Come in," Piety said. "We're really glad to see you."

A number of people were talking in the hall of the house, and they smiled at me as I walked past.

"These are pilgrims as well. We take care of them," Charity explained.

"It's not quite time for supper," Discretion said to her sisters, "so why don't you let Christian tell you all about his journey."

The three girls led me to a large room, where a lamp cast its cheerful light on the walls that were covered with pictures.

"If you're not too tired to talk," Piety said, "we really would like to hear about your journey. What made you leave your home?"

"I was too frightened to stay," I said. "The visitors who came to our city used to tell us it would be destroyed, and we were in great danger."

"And why did you think of coming into the Way of the King?"

I knew exactly why. "I read about the King and his Son in my Book, and one day Evangelist met me and showed me the way to the Wicket Gate."

I told the sisters about Obstinacy and Pliable, about the Slough of Despond, young Worldly-Wiseman, and Goodwill at the Wicket Gate.

Charity brought a footstool and sat down near me. She reminded me a bit of Christiana. Charity's name meant "Caring love," and I was starting to see that there was a good reason for everyone's names. These four sisters girls probably spent their time helping their guests.

"Did you visit the house of Interpreter?" Charity asked.

"Oh, yes," I replied enthusiastically. "He showed me so many things. There was a filthy room that no one could clean by sweeping it. The dust flew everywhere when the floor was swept, making everything much worse. But it was quickly washed clean with water."

"Why was that?" Prudence asked.

I knew why. "Interpreter said it's like our hearts that need to be washed clean by the King's Son. I saw a picture of the Good Shepherd, and I saw a boy fussing to have all his presents now. One of the best things I saw was a fire that the King's enemy tried to put out with water. But the King's Son was standing behind the fire, putting oil on the flames to make sure they stayed burning brightly."

I paused, and the three sisters just looked at me, as though wanting me to explain this.

"I suppose it's like our lives once we start to follow the King," I said. "He will keep us burning for him, even though his enemy tries to stop us. Then I watched a soldier fight his way into a palace. I spent the night there, but I wish I could have stayed longer."

The three girls were laughing, but not unkindly. I think they were amused by the way I told everything in such a rush.

"And what have you done today?" Prudence asked, as soon as I got my breath back.

"First, I passed by the Cross, and there I lost my burden. I even thought I saw the King's Son on that Cross for a moment. But it was empty. The King's Son forgave me for everything I've ever done wrong. Look at these new clothes the King gave me. I also had a Roll of Faith with a message from the King, and this mark on my forehead."

Prudence nodded. "You've had a busy day."

"That's not all. I found three boys sleeping on the grass by the side of the road. I tried to wake them, but they wouldn't listen to me. Then two boys called Formality and Hypocrisy climbed over the wall, but I think they chose the wrong paths when we came to Hill Difficulty, because that was the last I saw of them." I felt even more out of breath by this time.

"This hill is hard to climb," Piety said.

"You're right," I agreed. "I thought I was never going to get to the top. And when I saw the lions in the darkness I nearly turned back, but Watchful called to me and told me they were chained."

"Do you ever think about your old home?" Prudence asked.

I sighed. "Sometimes."

Prudence smiled. "Have you ever wished you were back there?"

"Once or twice, when I've been tired. But I'm sure the Celestial City is far better than the City of Destruction, and I know I'll be happy when I get there."

"Why will you be happy?" Prudence asked. I think she knew the answer, and was just testing me.

"Because I'll see the King's Son," I told her. "It was cruel of those people to nail him to the Cross, and I love him because he let himself be punished instead of me, so the King will never be angry with me again."

Prudence nodded and smiled, saying nothing. I knew I'd given the right answer.

"Do you have any family?" Charity asked.

"My mother's with the King in his City," I said, "and my father..."

Charity guessed I'd stopped for a good reason. "I suppose he's too busy to come," she said.

I nodded. "Do you think he'll *always* be busy, or will he be able to come too?"

"I can't tell," Charity said thoughtfully. "Perhaps when he knows that you and your mother are so happy, he'll want to be with you and begin his pilgrimage."

"If he comes, please tell him I stayed here, so when he gets to the Gates of the Celestial City he'll be able see me watching for him."

"We will," Charity promised. "And do you have any special friends?"

"Yes, I know a girl called Christiana, but she's still in the City of Destruction." I thought for a moment. "She was a good friend. We spent a lot of time together, and I wish she was here with me now."

"Why didn't you bring her with you?" Charity asked. "You would have someone to talk to on the Way."

"She didn't believe what the visitors said," I explained. "Anyway, she has four brothers to take care of. Their parents are living in the Celestial City, and Christiana has to do everything herself."

Charity frowned. "Didn't you talk to her, and beg her to come with you?"

"I often told her about the King but, you know, I might not have come myself if Evangelist hadn't shown me the Way. I started out so quickly I didn't even find her to say goodbye."

"Well, perhaps Evangelist will find her, and she'll bring her brothers with her."

At this moment the supper bell rang. I felt hungry as well as weary, and I enjoyed the good food that was set before me. After supper the oldest sister, Discretion, took me upstairs to a pleasant room with a window looking towards the east, and I soon fell asleep after such a tiring day.

CHAPTER 16
The Armory

In the morning, Discretion took me to one side. "I think it will do you good to stay with us for a few days," she said.

"I'd like to stay," I told her, "if I'm not in the way."

She smiled. "You won't be in the way at all, Christian. Taking care of pilgrims is part of the work we do for the King, and we're always glad to have young pilgrims staying at the house. Now, I have many things to do, so my sisters will take you into the library."

I spent a happy day at the House Beautiful, looking through books and documents with the three youngest sisters.

"This is the King's Son," Piety said, opening a large book. "You must have read in your Book how he came from the Celestial City to live in the City of Destruction, and was a baby in a poor home. Here he is in the arms of his mother, and the shepherds are kneeling round him."

Other books showed why the King's Son had died on the Cross, to make this special path to safety in the Celestial City.

Part 1 - Christian's Journey

Sometimes Charity was with me, sometimes Prudence and sometimes Piety.

The time passed so quickly that I was surprised when evening came. Discretion had been busy all day, but before the lamps were lit she came into the library where I was reading. I put my book down and she sat with me, telling many good things about the King and his Son.

"I've never spent such a happy day in all my life," I said to Discretion, when it was time for bed. "If I didn't want to live in the King's City, I'd like to stay here for ever."

* * *

I spent three whole days at the House Beautiful learning about the King, for there was so much I didn't know. On the second day Discretion allowed me to see the armory, a storeroom containing all kinds of weapons for use by the King's followers.

Here I saw rows of shining helmets, shields, breastplates of the finest metal, glittering swords, and shoes that Charity told me would never wear out.

I couldn't help thinking how much I would like to have a sword and shield of my own, and be one of the King's soldiers.

Piety sat down by the window in the armory, and told me about the wonderful things some of the King's soldiers had done. She told me about a boy called David, who had fought with a great giant.

"The giant was one of the King's enemies," Piety explained, "and he thought he could kill David easily. The giant was covered with armor from head to foot, and David wore only a shepherd's clothes and carried neither sword nor spear."

"What did he fight with?" I asked, puzzled as to why anyone would try to fight a giant without any sort of weapon.

"He had a sling and a stone and, when he threw the stone at the giant, the King helped him. He aimed it so well that he struck the giant on the forehead and killed him. Then he cut off the giant's head."

This story reassured me, for if the King had helped David, I felt certain he would be ready to help any other pilgrim who trusted in him.

In another book I read about a pilgrim called Little-Faith, who went to sleep by the side of the Way. As he was waking up, three brothers called Faint-heart, Mistrust and Guilt, robbed him. Then, because the brothers thought someone was coming, they ran away. Little-Faith was safe, but all he had left was his Roll of Faith and a few other things the King had given him. that reminded me how I'd lost my Roll of Faith earlier, and I quickly checked that I still had it.

On the third day, I said to Prudence, "Is it time for me to go on with my journey?"

"Not yet," Prudence said. "It's misty this morning, and you haven't seen the view from the tower on top of the house. We'll have to wait for the mist to clear."

So I spent another happy and peaceful day.

The next morning, when I opened my bedroom window, I saw that the mist had cleared. As soon as breakfast was over the three youngest sisters took me up to the top of the house. Far away in the distance I could see a long range of hills, with broad green fields and vineyards, and shady woods. I could

Part 1 - Christian's Journey

even pick out streams sparkling in the sunlight as they flowed into the quiet valleys.

"Oh," I said, "what a pleasant country that must be."

"That's Immanuel's Land," Piety explained. "The Way of the King passes through it. The hills are called the Delectable Mountains, and that's where you have to go. There are some shepherds there, who often help the pilgrims passing that way. If you ask them, they'll probably be able to take you high up into the mountains and show you the Gates of the Celestial City."

That sounded exciting. "Will it take me long to get there?" I asked.

"I don't know," Piety said. "You're a young pilgrim, and you can't travel fast."

Just then we heard Discretion calling us. "We must let Christian start in good time," she said. "He needs to reach the valley before the sun gets too hot."

"I'm ready to leave straight away," I began, but Charity interrupted me.

"No you're not. There's something we have for you."

"There certainly is," Discretion said, and she led the way to the armory. "Between this house and the Celestial City the King's enemies can be dangerous, and all pilgrims should carry weapons."

I glowed with pleasure when I found I was to have some armor of my own.

"I want to see you made into a soldier," Charity said, and I wished Christiana could have been there to see me.

Discretion chose a helmet and breastplate of the right size. "Always keep them bright and shining," she said.

Then Piety brought me a shield, which was large enough to protect me, but not too heavy to carry.

Prudence fastened a sword at my side, and Charity fitted on my shoes. I had nothing to protect my arms and legs, but I knew I could use the shield. The only part of me at risk was my back.

When I was finally ready, Discretion said quietly, "May the blessing of the King go with you, Christian, and may you continue to be his faithful soldier and servant to the end of your life."

I was too happy to say anything, but Discretion seemed to understand how I felt.

"I have one more gift for you," she said, handing me a small silver key. "It is called the Key of Promise. There are many promises engraved on it, but you cannot see them all at the same time. Look, there is a promise there now."

The letters were small, but I read the words aloud. *"I have come as Light into the world, so that everyone who believes in me will not remain in darkness."*

Discretion nodded. "That promise comes from the King's Son," she said. "One day you may be in darkness and need that promise – urgently!"

I thanked the sisters for their kindness.

"You must thank the King," Discretion said. "He is the one who gives you all these things."

CHAPTER 17
Apollyon the Destroyer

Watchful stood at the door of his lodge as I came out of the House Beautiful. As he opened the gates for me to leave, Discretion asked him if he'd seen any other pilgrims passing by.

"I saw one not long ago," the gatekeeper said. "He told me his name is Faithful."

I felt excited. "I know Faithful," I said excitedly. "He lived near me in the City of Destruction. We used to talk about what's in my Book, but he always said he'd think about it later. I'm so glad he started out. Is he far ahead?"

"It is about half an hour since I saw him," Watchful told me. "I should think by this time he will be at the bottom of the Hill."

Perhaps Faithful had spoken to Evangelist, and now he too was a pilgrim. I was so pleased at the thought of having a companion, that I made up my mind to walk as quickly as possible in order to meet with Faithful. But first I had to say goodbye to my friends, who had all come to the gates with me.

"It's such a beautiful morning," Discretion said to her sisters. "Let's walk down the Hill with Christian."

"Perhaps we'll see Faithful there," Charity added. "I wonder why he didn't come in to see us."

Discretion smiled. "It's early. I expect he wanted to hurry on with his journey."

The House Beautiful was right on the top on top of Hill Difficulty. I could see a valley below, and the path leading down from the gates of the house looked steep indeed.

"It's difficult to get up the Hill, and dangerous to go down," I said, more to myself than to the others.

Prudence heard me. She nodded. "People sometimes have bad falls on this path, after resting at our house."

She spoke the truth. Maybe because I wasn't yet used to carrying my sword and shield, I kept slipping and falling until I was aching all over. I was relieved when we reached the valley, where Discretion gave me a bag of food and something to drink on my way.

"We've been glad to see you," she said, "and I won't forget to give your message to your father if he comes to the House Beautiful."

I was sorry to say goodbye, and when Discretion and her sisters had left me, I felt so alone – as well as bruised. The valley was quiet and cool, and I walked on quickly hoping to see Faithful in the distance. But instead of finding Faithful, I saw ahead of me a hideous monster with scales like a fish, wings like a dragon, feet like a bear, and out of his body came fire and smoke. His mouth was like the mouth of a lion.

Part 1 - Christian's Journey

My first thought was to turn round and run back towards Hill Difficulty. Discretion or one of her sisters might see me, or perhaps Watchful would be at the house gates and send someone to help. I had my breastplate and shield, but they would be no use unless I *faced* my enemy. So I determined to trust in the King and go straight on. Perhaps, as I was young, the creature would pass by without taking any notice.

I walked on steadily, and a minute later the thing was close.

"My name is Apollyon," the monster roared, blocking the path and looking down at my bright shield and breastplate. "They call me the Destroyer, and I would like to know where you've come from."

I was scared, but I managed to say, "From a bad place. From the City of Destruction."

"And where are you going?"

"To a much better place. To the City of the King."

The Destroyer laughed loudly. "Perhaps you don't know that the City of Destruction belongs to me, so you belong to me as well. You have a choice. Either come back with me now, or I will kill you here."

"It doesn't matter if the city belongs to you," I said, trying to sound brave. "The King loves me better than you do, and I belong to him now."

The Destroyer smiled. "Don't be so foolish. I can be kind to people when I like them, and if you come back with me, and promise not to run away again, I won't be angry with you. You can live in my house and be one of my servants."

I shook my head firmly. "I'm one of the *King's* servants. I've sworn my allegiance to him. So how can I go back and not be a traitor?"

"Oh, that doesn't matter," the Destroyer said, still smiling. "The King's servants often run away. Besides, you were my friend when you were at home, which is why I'm willing to forgive you and take you back again."

I felt my knees shake, but I answered, "I didn't know I was your servant at the time. I realize it now, but I love the King, and I'd rather be *his* servant than yours. Now, let me go on my way."

The King's enemy had obviously made up his mind that I would go home with him. "Don't be in such a hurry," he said in a voice that sounded almost kind. "Just think of all the trouble you'll meet on the Way. My soldiers are up and down everywhere, and if they see you and try to hurt you, I don't suppose the King will bother to help."

"He will," I said boldly. "I only have to call to him."

"He won't bother with *you*," the Destroyer roared. "You know you've served the King badly since you set out. You were so careless that you even fell into the Slough of Despond. Then you let young Worldly-Wiseman deceive you and turn you out of the right path. How can you be sure you lost your burden at the Cross? You slept in the shelter on Hill Difficulty and nearly lost your Roll of Faith. When you saw the lions you were going to turn back, you were so afraid. And yet, at the House Beautiful, you talked as if you were one of the King's most *faithful* servants. I don't know how you can expect the King to do anything for *you!*"

I knew that all these things were true, and wondered how the Destroyer had heard about them.

"I've told the King I'm sorry," I said. "And he's forgiven me."

Suddenly the Destroyer became fierce with rage. "I hate your King and I hate his Son!" he cried. "And I hate everybody and everything belonging to him. You're *my* servant, Christian, and you'll *never* get to the Celestial City – because I'm going to kill you!"

CHAPTER 18
"Take Courage!"

I only just had time to put up my shield before the Destroyer started hurling fiery darts at me. There were so many they clattered against my shield like hail. Then I remembered the story I'd heard at the House Beautiful, of David and the giant, and I thought, "David only had his shepherd's clothes, and I have the King's sword and shield. I'll trust in him, and try not to be afraid. I belong to the King now."

So I held my shield firmly on my arm and deflected nearly all the Destroyer's darts, although some hit my hands and feet. Then the evil enemy became wild with fury. Rushing at me, he seized me in his strong claws, cutting into my arms and legs, making me bleed so much that I began to feel faint.

The Destroyer saw this, and he flung me to the ground. I thought he was going to kill me. I'd already drawn my sword from its sheath, but when the Destroyer threw me down it had fallen from my hand. As I lay on the path I thought I had no chance of escaping from this cruel enemy.

Part 1 - Christian's Journey

Just as the Destroyer was going to strike his last blow, I called to the King. At that moment I remembered some words in my Book spoken by the King's Son. *"Take courage, I have overcome the world."* Then I saw that the sword lay within my reach. I put out my hand and caught it up, and before the Destroyer had time to prevent me, I thrust it deep into his body.

The King's enemy couldn't bear the pain of a wound given with one of the King's swords, and he screamed loudly as I struck him. Then my courage returned, and I thrust the weapon at my enemy a second time. With a hideous roaring, the Destroyer fled across the valley leaving me alone.

I lay for a minute on the path, then got up slowly and painfully to look around. The King's enemy was gone, but all over the grass I could see the sharp darts he had thrown at me.

"It was the King who helped me," I thought, and my heart was full of thankfulness.

But I knew I'd been badly wounded, and I felt weak. I fell onto the grass and rested my head against a great rock. After a few minutes I fell asleep, and as I slept I dreamt that the King's Son was with me, rubbing my wounds with healing leaves.

When I woke up, my arms and legs had stopped bleeding and didn't even ache. Then I remembered that Discretion had given me something to eat and drink, so I sat still for a while and refreshed myself.

"I must hurry," I thought as I finished my meal. "I've lost so much time. I wonder if the Destroyer has gone for good, or if he'll come back to look for me again. He said his soldiers are always around, so I must be ready to meet them."

Keeping my sword in my hand, and looking carefully from side to side among the rocks and bushes, I continued along the Way of the King. The words of a song came to my mind, and I began to sing it:

>"The Valiant-for-Truth man
>By handling Sword and Shield,
>Doth make an evil dragon,
>Quit the field."

Part 1 - Christian's Journey

CHAPTER 19
The Dark Valley

It was late in the afternoon when I came to the end of the valley. I had seen nothing more of my enemy, and was beginning to think that I might now put my sword back into its sheath, when I saw two boys running towards me.

"Where are you going?" I asked, for they looked terrified.

"Back, back!" they shouted. "And you'll go with us if you value your life!"

"Why, what's the matter?"

"Matter?" they said, shaking with fear. "We were going the same way as you to the Celestial City, but we only just turned back in time to prevent being killed."

"Tell me what you saw?" I said, wondering if they had met the Destroyer.

"We were nearly at the Dark Valley," one of the boys said, "and then we saw it ahead."

"Saw what?" I asked anxiously, for I was now sharing their panic.

"Why, the valley itself. It's as dark as pitch. We saw all sorts of terrible creatures, and heard howling and yelling. All over the Dark Valley hang the clouds of uncertainty. Death was there, too, spreading its wings. In a word, it was horrible."

"Well," I said, "that's the way I have to go."

They couldn't persuade me to turn round, and I couldn't persuade them to go with me. So we parted, and I went on with my sword ready in my hand.

As the darkness closed around me, I caught sight of a deep ditch on one side, and an area of marshland more dangerous than the Slough of Despond on the other. A thick mist now swirled around my path, hiding it from sight. I could only just see my hand when I stretched it out in front of my face, and at times I had no idea where I was putting my feet.

Flames and smoke poured from the ground, while flashes of light and terrible cries came out from the rocks above. Someone came up behind me and whispered unpleasant words about the King's Son in my ear. To my horror I thought I was saying these words myself, and I wondered how I could be so bad as to even think such things. I realized later I should have put my fingers in my ears and talked to the King's Son, but at the time I had no idea where the words were coming from.

I wondered whether to turn round, for I was becoming so frightened that my whole body started shaking. I sensed some evil soldiers marching closer and closer. There was only one thing to do now: I called out to the King to give me his strength to go on through the blackness.

I had already come a long way through this valley, and I said to myself, "Perhaps I'm not far from the end of it, and going back might be worse than going forward." So I said loudly, "I will walk in the strength of the King."

Presently I found that the soldiers had taken a different path, and I didn't meet them at all. At that moment I heard someone young repeating words that were in my Book. "Even though I walk through the Valley of the Shadow of Death, I fear no evil, for you are with me." Only someone who was one of the King's pilgrims could say those words, but I had no chance of seeing anybody in this thick mist.

CHAPTER 20
Faithful

In spite of my tiredness, I walked on through the mist and darkness, all the time calling to the King to watch over me, and occasionally hearing someone ahead repeating words from my Book.

It was getting light now, and when I looked back I was shocked to see just how dangerous the valley had been. The deep ditch on one side, and the marsh on the other, filled me with horror when I saw how close I had come to disaster. I thought I saw a dragon slinking back into the shadow of the rocks, and evil figures disappearing as the sun rose.

Then I looked forward, and felt more and more thankful that the sun had risen, for the path ahead was, if possible, even more dangerous. From where I was, right to the end of the valley, the Way was so covered with snares, traps and nets, and so full of deep holes, that if it been dark I would never have survived the night.

I soon came to a small hill, where pilgrims could look ahead and see the path they had to take. As I reached the top, I caught sight of a young pilgrim not far away. I called out to him, but my voice only made him hurry away.

"Stop," I called. "Wait for me."

The pilgrim turned and shouted, "Not on my life. The enemy is coming."

I didn't know if he was referring to me, or the enemy in the Dark Valley, but I ran as fast as I could and quickly caught up with him. But in my rush I raced past, unable to stop. The next thing I knew I was flat on my back on the ground.

The young pilgrim laughed as he helped me to my feet. "I'm not laughing at you," he said, "but at myself for thinking you were some terrible fiend!"

Once he'd cleared that up, we walked together. He said his name was Faithful, and he was going to the Celestial City. I told him I thought it would be a good idea if we traveled together.

"I remembered things you told me from your Book," Faithful said as we walked along. "I wanted to leave the City of Destruction with you, but you left in such a hurry that I didn't know you'd gone. So I've been walking by myself."

"Did you stay long?" I asked.

He shook his head briefly. "Only a few days. Everybody i talking about you, and I kept wishing I'd left the city when you did."

"What were people saying about me?" I asked, surprised that anybody had even noticed I'd gone.

Faithful looked slightly embarrassed. "Well," he said, "if you must know, most of them are saying you're stupid."

"I don't mind. That's what they kept telling me when I lived there," I said with a laugh. "What happened to Pliable?"

"When his friends heard he'd only got as far as the Slough of Despond, they jeered at him for not going on."

"That's strange," I said, frowning. "They're laughing at me because I went on, and they're laughing at Pliable because he went back."

Faithful shrugged. "I think Pliable is seven times worse than he was before he set out. Anyway, I crossed the Slough safely without getting stuck, but before I reached the Wicket Gate I met a girl who tried to persuade me go with her to her village near Mount Law. In the end she walked off, saying I was a waste of her time."

I remembered how I'd met young Worldly-Wiseman at the same place. Perhaps there was often someone there, trying to try to stop people from reaching the Wicket Gate. I said, "You must be glad you didn't listen to her. Did you meet anyone else?"

"Not there. I got through the Wicket Gate without any problems, but when I came to Hill Difficulty I saw an old man sitting by the side of the road. He told me I had an honest face, and offered to take me back to his home in the town of Deceit. He said I could marry one of his daughters when I'm older. He even told me I could have all his riches when he died. He was so pleasant that I couldn't help listening, and he almost persuaded me to go with him."

"Oh," I cried, "he would have made you into his slave."

Part 1 - Christian's Journey

Faithful nodded. "I can see that now. I was just about to turn back when I saw he was smiling to himself in a nasty way. So I said, 'I won't go.' That made him angry, and he told me he'd send someone to punish me. But I escaped and went up Hill Difficulty."

"Did he send anyone after you?" I asked.

"Well, certainly someone came after me. Just as I was passing the shelter, I heard a man running up the hill as fast as the wind. He shouted that he'd come to punish me for listening to the old man. He knocked me to the ground and hit me so many times that I pleaded for mercy. He told me his name was Justice, and he wasn't allowed to be kindhearted. I thought he was going to kill me. At that moment a man with a gentle face came by, and he told Justice not to strike me."

I had a sudden idea who this was. "Did he tell you his name?

"I didn't know who it was at first, but when he was going up the hill I saw nail marks on his feet and his hands, and I'm sure it was the King's Son."

"I've heard about Justice," I said, "and I'm glad I didn't meet him."

Faithful nodded and smiled. "In a way I'm glad I did," he said. "He helped me understand just how much the King's Son loves us, because he let Justice punish him instead of punishing me."

CHAPTER 21
Talkative

We were just entering a wilderness, a large expanse of flat land, when we heard someone coming our way. We turned quickly to see a young man waving.

"Are you going to the Celestial City?" Faithful called to him.

The young man hurried towards us. "Indeed I am," he said.

"Then we can talk together as we travel," Faithful told him.

The young man hesitated. "Much depends what you wish to talk about," he said. "Talking can sometimes be nothing but a costly waste of time."

"What would you like to talk about?" Faithful asked, looking a little put out.

The young man drew himself up tall. "I will talk of heavenly things, or earthly things; of moral things, or evangelical things; of sacred things, or irreverent things; of things in the past, or things to come; of foreign things, or things at home – anything, as long as it is worthwhile."

I recognized this young man. If he was going to carry on like this all the way to the Celestial City, the journey would indeed seem long. I drew Faithful to one side. "Don't you know recognize him?"

Faithful shook his head.

"As far as I know, he still lives in the City of Destruction," I said quietly. "His name is Talkative."

Faithful shrugged. "I've never seen him there."

"Well," I said, "the city is a large place. But he's not a pleasant person."

Faithful looked annoyed. "He seems all right to me," he mumbled.

"Not when you get to know him. He's like a painting that looks fine from a distance, but when you're close you can see it's not so good. Talkative will say so many things, depending on what he thinks we want to hear. He'll talk about prayer, repentance, faith and new birth. But that's all he can do. He has knowledge in his head, but not in his heart."

For the next thirty minutes Talkative bored us with details of his extensive knowledge. Without doubt, he knew a lot more than I did about the King, but it didn't seem to mean much to him.

At last Faithful pulled me aside. "I was prepared to welcome Talkative's companionship at first," he said quietly, "but I'm sick of him already. What shall we do to get rid of him?"

"Mention something about the love the King and his Son have for us," I suggested. "And listen carefully to what he says."

So Faithful listened, while his companion talked endlessly about the King's goodness. When I moved nearer, Faithful said to Talkative, "I suppose you are careful to obey the King?"

Talkative looked away. I wasn't surprised, because he always did just what he liked, but was ready to tell other people what he thought the King had commanded *them* to do.

"I don't see that it matters to you," he said angrily.

"I think it *does* matter," Faithful said. "If you talk so much about loving the King, you ought to serve him."

"How do you know that I don't serve him?" Talkative snapped back.

"Do you?" Faithful asked pointedly.

"Don't you talk to me like that," Talkative shouted. "I'm older than you are."

Faithful looked stunned by this reply. "I only want to be sure you're a real pilgrim. That's all."

"A real pilgrim? Of course I am. But I know what's going on." Talkative glared at me, his eyes flashing. "Christian has been telling you a lot of stories about me, and I suppose you believe them all."

Faithful said nothing, but walked on quietly with me.

"I don't care," Talkative called, dropping back. "Since you only want to believe bad things about me, I wouldn't want to walk with you anyway. And so adieu."

With that, he walked off quickly, back along the way we'd just come.

"Never mind," Faithful said to me. "To tell you the truth, Christian, I'm glad he hasn't stayed with us. I don't think he'd have done us any good."

"You're right," I agreed. "But perhaps he'll think about what we've said, and I hope one day he'll start his journey in the right way."

Faithful laughed. "We may even see him in the Celestial City." And in spite of his smile, I knew he was serious. The King would welcome *anyone* who wanted to come to him and follow him.

CHAPTER 22
Warnings

By the time we left Talkative behind, we were nearly out of the wilderness. The Way of the King went straight ahead, and as I looked along it I was glad to have Faithful for company.

I turned round to see how far we'd come, and saw a man hurrying towards us. "It's Evangelist," I shouted in excitement, pleased to see my friend again. I was so grateful that he'd taken the time to talk to me in the City of Destruction and help me start my journey, but I'd not had a chance to thank him properly since then.

It seemed a long time ago that I'd become stuck in the Slough of Despond, and as soon as Evangelist caught up with us I told him all the things that had happened to me, including the mistakes I'd made.

Evangelist smiled. "I'm glad to hear that the King has brought you through everything safely, in spite of your sometimes failing him. And he will always help you."

"I'm sure he will," I agreed.

Then Evangelist turned to Faithful. "Tell me about your adventures," he said.

"I haven't fought any battles yet." Faithful looked embarrassed, and seemed half-afraid to speak.

Evangelist obviously noticed this. "You love and trust the King with all your heart," he told Faithful. "I'm sure you'll be just as brave as Christian, if the servants of the evil prince attack you."

Faithful said he hoped he would be.

"Sometimes people have to suffer much," Evangelist continued. "Remember, if you are faithful unto death, the King will give you a crown of life."

It was only later that I realized what Evangelist was saying. But from the look on Faithful's face, he understood the meaning of those words.

"Tell us more about the road," I begged. "Will it be easier now, or are there other frightening places to pass through?"

Evangelist looked serious. "I came to meet you here," he told us, "because you are approaching the gates of Vanity Fair, a great town built by the evil prince many thousands of years ago. It looks like a beautiful place, full of all kinds of pleasant things, but most of the people there will hate you."

"Maybe there won't be a fair today," Faithful said.

Evangelist explained that there was never a single day when it wasn't possible to buy whatever people wanted in Vanity Fair. "You can buy and sell silver, gold, pearls, precious stones, houses, land, goods, titles, countries, kingdoms and any sort of pleasure all through the year."

"Do we *have* to pass through it?" Faithful asked, sounding more than a little anxious. He'd been extremely quiet since Evangelist mentioned the crown of life.

"All pilgrims going to the Celestial City have to travel through Vanity Fair," Evangelist said. "Even the King's Son had to pass through, and the evil prince tried to make him buy some of its wares."

"But we don't have to stay there, do we?" I asked, seeing a way out of our problems.

Evangelist shook his head. "No, you don't. Just remember that you mustn't stop. Unfortunately, some pilgrims decide to stay to look round. Then, when they've been in the town a few days, they forget the King altogether. When they see other pilgrims passing on their way to the Celestial City, they try to persuade them to stay with them."

"What shall we do?" Faithful asked. I could tell he was afraid of the place, and couldn't help wondering how brave he would be if we had trouble there.

Evangelist laid a hand on Faithful's shoulder. "Walk quietly along the streets. Don't stop to look at the things in the shops and in the market. Some days the townspeople leave pilgrims alone, but there are times when they treat them badly."

"Might they even *kill* us?" I asked. It was my turn to sound anxious.

"There have been times when they've been evil enough to kill people who won't serve their prince," Evangelist said. "But don't be fearful. If you do have to die there, the King will send his angels to carry you to be with him for ever."

Part 1 - Christian's Journey

The sun was just setting when Evangelist said goodbye, and before its light faded we saw the walls and gates of a great town in the distance.

"Are you scared?" I asked Faithful.

"Not very," he said hesitantly, but I think he was. "The King's Son will take care of us, and you have your sword and shield."

"If you'd stayed at the House Beautiful you would have been given some armor, too."

"Never mind," Faithful said, with a quick smile. "I'll keep close to you, and if the people *do* kill me, there will be no more enemies to fight."

We passed through the wide archway just as darkness fell. The heavy gates slammed shut behind us. We were locked inside Vanity Fair.

CHAPTER 23
Vanity Fair

I spent the night with Faithful sleeping in a sheltered corner, just inside the gates. When he built Vanity Fair, the evil prince must have known that when pilgrims reached the town they'd be feeling tired and faint, and he'd be hoping to persuade them to stay here instead of going on to the Celestial City.

As soon as the sun rose, we began our walk through the town. I thought that if we started early, we might be able to reach the opposite gate before the streets became crowded with people.

The evil prince had filled the place with everything that looked pleasant and beautiful. There were broad streets and handsome houses, and the stalls in its market were full of glittering wares. People passed busily up and down wearing fine clothes, spending their whole time pleasing themselves. Clearly the evil prince took care to give them plenty of things to enjoy. They seemed to have not a moment to spare in which to think of the King they had ignored.

Part 1 - Christian's Journey

"We won't go into any houses," I said. "Evangelist warned us not to get involved with anyone here."

But my bright shield and breastplate, and Faithful's new clothes, weren't like those worn by the people in Vanity Fair. We'd only gone a short distance when some men who were strolling by called out, "Look at those two pilgrims! Let's go after them and stop them!"

We heard them running up behind us, but we didn't look round.

"Don't take any notice," I said to Faithful. "Perhaps they'll not bother us."

But when the men came up, they crowded round us and refused to let us pass.

"Tell us where you've come from," one said.

"And who gave you that shield and those silly clothes?" another demanded.

"Why don't you look at the shops?" a third asked. "What do you want to buy from us? How about buying some proper clothes?"

"Someone like you doesn't need a sword and a shield," one stallholder called to me. "Sell them, and buy something worth having. And you," he said, pointing at Faithful, "wear something different. The King's clothes make you look ridiculous."

Faithful shook his head, "These are the King's clothes, and we don't need any of your goods. We're going to the Celestial City."

This made the people jeer, and one man pushed Faithful so hard that he would have fallen if I'd not been holding him.

By this time a gang of children had run towards us, and some older people stopped to discover the reason for all the noise. Then I saw one of the evil prince's servants pushing his way towards us. The man must have seen my shining helmet, so he would know we were pilgrims. I watched him making his way quickly through the crowd.

"What are you doing?" he demanded, as he seized us by our shoulders. "Our prince doesn't allow fighting in the streets."

"We're not fighting," I said. "We were walking along quietly."

"That's nonsense," the man shouted. "I've been watching you causing a disturbance here in the market. You must come with me."

"We're the King's pilgrims," Faithful said boldly. "We're not disturbing anyone. We only want to pass through your town."

"I don't know anything about the King's pilgrims," the man retorted. "All I can see is that you're two foolish, troublesome young people, and you must be taken before the Governor."

So he led us down the street to the Governor's house, and the people of the town followed, laughing and making fun of us.

Part 1 - Christian's Journey

CHAPTER 24
The Governor

When Faithful and I were brought before the Governor of the town, he rubbed his hands together as though glad to have an excuse to punish someone who loved the King.

"We were doing nothing wrong," Faithful protested. "Some people in the town made fun of us, but we did nothing to them. There are plenty of people out there who can give evidence that we are innocent."

Somehow, I doubted there were any who would be willing to stand up for us.

"That's quite enough," the Governor said. "You are nothing but a nuisance, and you will both be beaten. Afterwards you will be shut in our jail, as an example to others, lest any should try to speak up for you, or think of becoming pilgrims too."

I knew it was no use saying anything in our defense, and when I heard the Governor say this, I felt very scared.

Faithful look pale, but he whispered to me, "If we die, we'll go straight to the King in the Celestial City. I shall think of the King, because I know he's with me."

A man came forward to beat us, and I remembered how I thought I'd seen the King's Son nailed to the Cross, and how he'd done it for me.

"The King's Son didn't mind the pain," I whispered, "and we mustn't mind it either, because we're the King's servants. It says in my Book that the King's servants are to be like his Son."

So although the strokes of the heavy cane on my back and legs made me want to scream, I tried not to cry out too loudly. Faithful behaved even more bravely.

The jail was a place in the middle of the market, with iron bars in front of it, looking like a cage for wild animals. After we'd been beaten, the jailer bound our hands and feet with chains, and the man who'd beaten us threw us into the cage and left us there.

I was unable to stand upright, I was in such pain. So I sat with Faithful, and we tried to comfort each other by retelling the King's promises.

"We knew they could be cruel," Faithful told me, "but it's for the King that we've been hurt. I'm glad I put up a good defense and refused to deny him as Lord and Master. He will always be with us."

When the people in the town heard that two of the King's pilgrims were lying in the cage they were eager to see us, and a crowd soon gathered round to stare and mock.

The people of Vanity Fair said all kinds of cruel things to upset us, and make us displease the King's Son by being hateful and furious with them. But we sat still, and neither of us gave an angry answer to anything they said.

Part 1 - Christian's Journey

At last some of the people, when they saw how patient we were, cried out, "Let them alone now. They've been beaten, and they've behaved bravely. Don't insult them any more."

But others seemed to enjoy seeing us suffer. So they went on taunting us until their companions grew angry with them, and before long there was a great disturbance in the market as the people who were sorry for us began to fight with those who were making fun.

The Governor came to see the cause of the disturbance, and commanded his men to stop the fighting. He ordered the men to beat us again, because he said the disturbance was our fault.

After our beating, the men threw us back into the cage.

CHAPTER 25
Judge Hate-Good

When the morning came, we were pulled from the cage. "Are you setting us free?" I asked the man who dragged us across the marketplace.

"Free?" the man jeered. "You're going to the Governor's Court. Judge Hate-Good sits specially to try prisoners like you. He's old, but he knows a pilgrim when he sees one. You two are in serous trouble. The judge can't stand the King."

With this, he laughed and pulled us along quickly. We stumbled forward to the courtroom with our legs in chains. Once there, Judge Hate-Good demanded to know what we'd been doing.

A boy named Envy, whom I recognized as one of the first to run after us and make fun, stood up to answer the judge's question. He said he'd known us when we were living in the City of Destruction, and we were disobedient and quarrelsome, and refused to honor the prince who was the ruler of their country.

Part 1 - Christian's Journey

Two men stood up, and agreed that what Envy said was true. They also told Judge Hate-Good they were afraid we'd do great harm to the young people of Vanity Fair if we were set free. They'd seen us laughing at the wonderful treasures with which their prince had filled the town, and saying they were not worth having, and pretending we knew of a finer city and another King whose laws were better than the laws of their prince.

I looked across the courtroom and saw twelve grim-faced men. They must be the jury whose duty it would be to listen to everything that was said about us, and then help Judge Hate-Good decide whether we deserved punishment or not. They were almost certainly chosen from among the chief servants of the evil prince, and were not likely to be fair to any of the King's pilgrims.

When Faithful asked if he might speak in his defense, the judge answered, "You ought to be put to death immediately for what you've done, but first we will hear what you have to say."

I wondered how it was that Faithful had become so brave. His face was white, but he no longer sounded frightened, even though the judge and the people in the court looked so spiteful.

Then Faithful began to answer, saying that he was against their prince who had set himself up as higher than the King. "As for the disturbance," Faithful said loudly, "we were not responsible for it. We came here in peace. The people of this town caused the trouble, because they couldn't bear to hear the truth about your prince."

"And what is the truth?" the Judge asked.

"Your prince is evil," Faithful said, "and I defy him and all his angels."

Judge Hate-Good turned to the jury with anger in his eyes, and said, "You have heard what Envy and his companions have told us about these two, and Faithful does not deny it. He refuses to serve our prince, and by the laws of our town he ought to be put to death."

Then the twelve men answered, "We can see that both these pilgrims are wicked, but Faithful is worse because he speaks against our prince. We say he must be killed, but Christian can be taken back to jail."

I was in such a panic about all that was happening that I barely took in what the men in the jury were saying. Then the soldiers led Faithful out of the court. Quickly they returned and took me to the cage in the marketplace, and from there I could see Faithful being beaten again. Some people started throwing stones as he fell to the ground. Then they rushed forward and kicked him.

"Oh, Faithful, Faithful," I called out, but Faithful didn't answer. He was looking up, his face shining.

And there, above the angry crowd, I saw a chariot and horses in the sky waiting for Faithful. Then, with a sound of trumpets, angels carried Faithful up through the clouds, leaving his broken body in the marketplace.

Part 1 - Christian's Journey

CHAPTER 26
Hopeful

I lay with my eyes closed for some time, feeling too weak to move or speak. Eventually I opened my eyes and realized I was no longer in the cage, but in a small room lying on a low bed, and a woman was bending over me. She was dressed like all the women in Vanity Fair, and although she didn't appear unkind, her face had a strange look that made me cautious.

"My husband is the man who keeps the jail," she explained. "When you fainted, the soldiers carried you from the marketplace, and I felt sorry for you."

She had a bowl of water, and bathed my hands and face, staying with me until I began to feel better.

"You're too young to be a pilgrim," she said. "I want to keep you here in this house and take care of you."

I knew I was right to be cautious. This woman was planning to stop me going on with my journey. "You've been kind to me," I said, "but I can't stay. I want to go to the King."

"I was going to the King once," the woman said, rather sadly, "but the Way was hard. Anyway, I've been happy enough in this town."

"You'd be happier with the King," I told her. "Faithful is with him already. I saw the King's angels waiting for him. And if they ever let me out of this place, I'm going to travel as fast as I can to the end of my journey."

The woman bent down closely to me, and I could see unhappiness in her eyes. "I was sorry when they told me about Faithful," she whispered, "but they're not going to kill you."

"I don't think I'd have minded if they had," I said. "I'd have gone straight to the Celestial City. Even if I'm allowed to continue, I'll be traveling on my own now Faithful is living with the King."

"They're only going to keep you for a few more days," the woman told me. "If you stay here with me, I promise I'll be kind to you."

I shook my head. "I can't stay. I love the King, and I must go to him."

After four days, the keeper of the jail told me that the governor of the town had given an order for me to be given my armor and set free, so I started once more on my journey. The jailor's wife told me she was sorry to see me go, and as I left she told me to think of her sometimes.

"I'll tell the King how you've helped me," I promised. "Perhaps you'll be a pilgrim again some day. If I see you coming into the Celestial City I'll recognize you."

Part 1 - Christian's Journey

The woman said nothing as I walked away. I went quietly down the street, not feeling strong enough to walk quickly, afraid the people would run after me as they'd done before. But because Faithful had been put to death, it seemed everyone was satisfied. Although some of the people laughed, they didn't touch or harm me in any way.

I was just passing through the great archway of the far town gate, when I felt a hand on my shoulder. For a moment I thought my troubles were beginning again, but the boy who had stopped me looked frightened, and said in a half-whisper, "Let me come with you, Christian. I don't want to stay here any longer."

"Are you a pilgrim too?" I asked in surprise.

"I was a pilgrim once. My name is Hopeful, and I hate this place. I've stayed here too long. I want to be a loyal pilgrim again."

CHAPTER 27
By-Ends

I left the town of Vanity Fair quickly, and although Hopeful kept close to me, he seemed afraid to say anything more

When we were clear of the town, Hopeful looked round anxiously. Seeing no one was close, he said, "Some of us were sorry when they killed Faithful. He was brave, and I'm sure he was good. Many people say they won't stay in Vanity Fair much longer if such cruel things are done there. I was passing the jailor's house when they let you go. You don't mind me coming, do you?"

"Not if you really love the King," I told him. "I was thinking I'd have to go the rest of the way by myself, so I'm glad to have company."

Hopeful smiled. "I wanted you to say that. I wasn't happy, and I always meant to run away some day."

I was about to ask Hopeful how long he'd been living in Vanity Fair, when we caught up with a boy about our age walking slowly on the sunny side of the road.

Part 1 - Christian's Journey

"I know him," Hopeful said quietly. "He's called By-Ends. He lives in the town of Fair-Speech not far from here. I don't think we can trust him."

"Why not," I asked.

"Well, the people who live there call themselves the King's servants, and pretend to love him. But By-Ends' name means he'll agree to anything to get what he wants. Whenever the evil prince or his servants go to his town, everyone leaves off talking about the King and behaves as if the evil prince is their ruler, so he will give them gifts."

"Why are there so many false pilgrims?" I asked, puzzled by what I kept finding. As far as I could see, there was nothing more exciting than following the Way to the King.

Hopeful shrugged. "I suppose they want an easy life. The evil prince isn't bothered about them. If any of them become pilgrims, he knows they'll soon turn back when they meet the smallest difficulty."

By-Ends walked with us for a short time. He told us he was a pilgrim, but he seemed more interested in telling us about his wealthy relations and friends in Fair-Speech than talking about the King. He certainly sounded proud of his high standing in that town. As he talked, the sun shone brightly, and the breeze felt soft and pleasant.

"It's a beautiful day," Hopeful said.

By-Ends smiled. "Just right for traveling. Of course, pilgrims from my town never start in the winter. We always choose the summer for our journeys. It's foolish to struggle against wind and rain."

"There are storms even in the summer," I said, interested to hear what By-Ends would say to that.

"Of course there are, but you needn't think I'm going to be stupid enough to travel in bad weather."

I shook my head. "I'm sure real pilgrims never mind about the weather."

That made By-Ends cross. "Let's not quarrel. If there's a storm, you can keep walking if you want to. I'll wait until it's over."

I'd read in my Book that it's not wise for pilgrims to travel closely with friends who aren't the King's true servants, so I said, "I'm sorry, but we'll not make good companions for you. We'll be keeping straight on, whether it's fine or stormy."

By-Ends pushed his hands into his pockets. "In that case you might as well go on by yourselves. I was happy enough strolling along before you came, and I'm sure I don't want either of you taking me anywhere difficult."

I wondered what to do. Maybe I could help By-Ends follow the Way to the King more closely if we stayed together. At that moment we heard people shouting behind, and turned to see three boys running towards us.

"They're my friends from Fair-Speech," By-Ends said in excitement. "They're the right sort of friends to have."

"By-Ends, where are you off to?" they shouted.

"There wasn't anything special to do at home," By-Ends said when they reached us, "so I thought I'd try being a pilgrim."

"We'll go with you. Who are these two?" they asked, pointing at Hopeful and me.

"Oh, these are pilgrims too," By-Ends told them, "but not *our* sort. I've been telling them I only travel while the weather keeps fine, so they don't want me walking with them. Anyway, I can't see the sense of plodding over rough roads in the wind and rain. It's much better to stop until the storm is over."

The three boys looked at us and laughed. "We know *your* sort," one of them jeered. "You can't do this and you can't do that – all because of your precious King!"

"He *is* precious," I agreed. "And, yes, I really want to follow him – because I know he loves me."

By-Ends turned to his friends. "See what I mean?" he said. "Come on, let's leave them to it. We can be a nice little group, traveling all by ourselves."

They stood together, laughing.

"It was a pity to upset By-Ends," I said to Hopeful, as we went on ahead, "but I don't see how we could help it. If we stayed with him, and there was a storm, he might talk us into turning back."

CHAPTER 28
The Silver Mine

By-Ends and his friends walked behind, talking and laughing loudly. I was soon far ahead with Hopeful, but presently the four boys ran and caught up with us, and began to ask questions.

They wanted to know if some of the things they liked doing were wrong, and likely to displease the King. I think they were hoping I wouldn't be brave enough to answer them truthfully, because they would then be able to call me a coward. But although I sometimes felt unsure of myself, I wasn't afraid to speak the truth. I was learning to love the King, and nothing these boys might do to me would make me agree with them.

I answered all their questions as well as I could, and at last they began to look ashamed of themselves and said no more. I was glad when they left us. I went on with Hopeful, while By-Ends and his three companions dropped behind again.

Soon we came to an open field where the pathway was smooth and easy. Something to the side caught our attention, and we turned to look. I noticed a dark opening in the hillside,

Part 1 - Christian's Journey

like the mouth of a cave. A boy stood on the hill, and he called to us.

"My name is Demas. Come up and see this."

"What is it?" I asked.

"It's a silver mine, and some people are already digging in it for treasure. With a little work, you may richly provide for yourselves."

"Come on," Hopeful said, "let's go and look."

But I pulled him back. "It's not a safe place. I think Demas is a servant of the evil prince. Why else would he invite people to help themselves to silver?"

I called to Demas and asked him if the mine was dangerous.

"It's safe, unless you're careless," Demas shouted back, but even from this distance I could seem his face going red.

"We could go back and have a quick look," Hopeful said wistfully.

I pulled him away. "I'm sure I've heard about this place. Anyway, we can't get to it without leaving the path."

"Don't worry," Demas called. "I can see four others coming behind you."

He'd seen By-Ends and his friends. We stayed to see what they would do, for they had no real love for the King. The four hurried up the hill and went to the mouth of the cave, and I wondered if they'd ever come out.

I pulled Hopeful by the arm. "We have to stop looking back," I said. "We must keep going."

When we'd walked for some distance beyond the hill, Hopeful stopped suddenly, saying, "Look at that. What is it?"

A white pillar stood by the side of the road. As we came nearer, we saw it was in the shape of a woman, with her face turned away from the Celestial City.

"Do you think she was a pilgrim?" Hopeful whispered.

"I don't think so," I said. "It looks like a statue. I wonder why it's here."

We walked round it, and studied it closely. Hopeful noticed some carved words. They were hard to read, and at first neither of us could make them out. But after puzzling over them a little, I read, "Remember Lot's Wife."

"I know what it is," I said. "I read about her in the library at the House Beautiful."

Then I told Hopeful how the King had once rescued a man named Lot, with his wife and two daughters, from a city that was being destroyed for its wickedness.

"The King sent an angel to bring the family out, and the angel told them not to look back. But Lot's wife *did* look back, because she was sad for what she was leaving behind, and the moment she turned she became a pillar of salt."

"What a dreadful thing," Hopeful said. "I was like her a few minutes ago, ready to look at the silver. I'm glad you stopped me turning back when Demas called us."

Part 1 - Christian's Journey

CHAPTER 29
The River of the Water of Life

Just as it was starting to get dark, we came to the bank of a broad river. A sign said it was the River of the Water of Life, where pilgrims could rest safely. It seemed a good place to stay, so we drank some cool, clear water from the river, which was pleasant and made us feel less tired.

Hopeful reached up for some fruit growing from one of the trees, and I picked a handful of the leaves and rubbed them gently into the wounds where I'd been beaten in Vanity Fair. Immediately I could feel the juice from the leaves soothing my cuts and bruises.

On each side of the river we saw a meadow covered in wild flowers. It seemed a safe place to rest, so we lay down and were soon fast asleep. We woke as the morning sun rose over the hills, and again ate some of the fruit and drank from the river.

That morning we bathed in the cool water, and I felt my whole body being refreshed. So there we rested in perfect safety, eating the fruit, and drinking the healing water.

After staying there for several nights, I felt fully recovered from my beatings in Vanity Fair, and ready to continue with the journey. But we stayed longer than necessary, simply because the place was so pleasant.

"I wonder if we're far from the Celestial City," I said early one morning, as the sun rose over the trees. "Come on, Hopeful, it's long past time we were on our way again."

Hopeful nodded in agreement. "Perhaps after this long rest we'll be able to travel faster than ever," he said, yawning.

I wasn't really looking forward to a long walk. Although the rest by the River of the Water of Life had done me good, I'd become lazy. I was hoping the path would be smooth and easy from now on.

Part 1 - Christian's Journey

CHAPTER 30
An Easy Path

We left the River of the Water of Life that morning, and traveled slowly along the Way of the King all day, our muscles aching from lack of walking. My legs felt tired and my back hurt. Late in the afternoon we came to a place where a stile led off into a broad, green meadow. A sign said By-Path Meadow. I recognized the name as meaning Two-Path Meadow, so probably one path was just as good as the other for pilgrims.

We'd already come a long way, and I felt too exhausted to go much further. The path leading from the river was rough and stony, and my feet were sore.

I stopped when I reached the stile, and leaned over it. A hedge divided the meadow from the Way of the King, and I could see a smooth, grassy path running close to it.

"Let's walk along this path for a little way," I suggested, turning to Hopeful. "The stones here are so hard they're hurting my feet."

"And mine," Hopeful said, "but I don't think that path is safe."

"Oh, it's all right," I said confidently. "Look, it runs close to the hedge. We'll be able to climb back onto the Way of the King whenever we want to."

Hopeful still seemed unhappy. "All right," he said at last, "if you're *sure* it's safe, I'll go with you."

We climbed over the stile into the meadow. The grass felt soft and pleasant to our feet, and not far in front we saw a man walking along by the hedge.

I called to him. "Can you tell us where this path leads?" Well, I wanted to be sure.

"To the Celestial City," the man said.

"There you are," I said to Hopeful. "I told you it was the right way." Then I called again to the man, "Who are you? May we walk with you?"

"My name is Vain-Confidence," the man said, stopping to talk, "but I'd rather walk by myself."

That struck me as rather unfriendly, but I told Hopeful we might as well follow Vain-Confidence. "And if there's any danger, we'll know in time to avoid it."

Hopeful still looked worried, and when night came, and the shadows grew so thick that we could no longer see Vain-Confidence, he told me he felt frightened.

Suddenly we heard a cry, and a sound like someone falling into a deep hole like a mine shaft. Hopeful seized my arm and clung to me, making me shake with fear from head to foot.

"What can have happened?" I asked. I called loudly to Vain-Confidence, but we received no answer, although we could hear someone groaning as if in terrible pain. Then the

Part 1 - Christian's Journey

sound stopped. Although we searched in the darkness, we were unable to find anyone.

"I'm sure we're not in the right way," Hopeful said, "but it's too dark to see anything."

I didn't answer. I knew I'd done wrong in climbing over the stile, and I wondered how I could have been so foolish to think that any path would be safe if it wasn't the Way of the King.

Then, before I could speak again, I felt heavy drops of rain on my face. A blinding flash of lightning darted across the sky, followed almost instantly by a roar of thunder. The rain poured in torrents, and the thunder and lightning were worse than anything I'd ever heard or seen before.

"How was I to know we were going the wrong way?" I muttered, but I knew it was all my fault. I turned to Hopeful, "I'm so sorry. I deserve to be in this danger, but you would never have come if I hadn't persuaded you."

"I might have done," Hopeful said. "I could have tried harder to stop you, but I thought you knew what you were doing, because you've been a better pilgrim than I have."

"Let's turn round," I said. "And let me go first in case we run into any more danger."

But Hopeful no longer trusted me, and insisted on leading the way back to the stile. By this time the heavy rain had already filled the streams that ran through the meadow, flooding the path by the hedge. In places the water was so deep that we could scarcely keep our footing, and I began to think we'd be drowned before we could get back to the Way of the King.

The storm lasted for several hours, and although we struggled on, we found it impossible to make our way back in the darkness. So at last we sat down under some dense bushes close to the hedge, and fell asleep.

Part 1 - Christian's Journey

CHAPTER 31
Giant Despair

I woke with a fright as a loud voice shouted, "What's that I see shining in the bushes?"

I caught sight of a giant striding through the long grass of the meadow, and he was coming our way. The giant must have seen my armor, even though it was badly splashed with the mud we'd walked through the night before.

"Who are you?" the giant called in a deep, booming voice.

I raised my head. The giant had shaggy hair and a rough beard, and clothes made of the skins of wild beasts. I cried out with fear, and this woke Hopeful who sprang up in alarm.

"What are you two doing on my land?" the giant demanded.

"We're pilgrims," I answered, feeling so afraid I could scarcely speak. "And we've lost our way."

"Is that so?" the giant bellowed. "You're trespassing here, and it looks as though you trampled over my crops last night. You must come along with me."

The storm was probably to blame for the damage to the giant's crops, but I knew that if we tried to run away he would catch us in a moment. The giant led us across the fields to his house, which had the name Doubting Castle above the massive doorway. Once inside, the giant threw us into a dark, stinking dungeon, and sat watching us.

Part 1 - Christian's Journey

Hopeful crept close to me and we sat together until the giant grew tired and went away. I was afraid he would lock us up for ever, and then we'd never reach the Celestial City.

Suddenly we heard a banging on the door of our dungeon, and a woman's voice said loudly, "My name is Diffidence. I am the wife of Giant Despair. My husband tells me he found you both sleeping in his meadow. Oh, how pleased I am to know that you're locked securely in here. My husband is coming to beat you without mercy. And then he'll beat you again. Ah, here he is now. My, what a large stick he has to hit you with." And she screeched with laughter.

After he had beaten us almost unconscious, Giant Despair left us again in the dark. We felt so bruised from the heavy blows that we lay on the ground twisting and turning in pain for most of the night.

The next day Despair visited us again, and seemed surprised to find us still alive. He told us he wanted us dead soon, but if we didn't wish to die by starving to death, we could drink some of the poison he was leaving with us.

I begged Giant Despair to set us free. This made him so angry that open the prison door and rushed at us with his stick. I think he would have killed us, but he fell down in a fainting fit and lay on the ground unable to move.

Giant Despair's wife was watching from the shadows. She slammed the door shut, and the evil grin on her face faded quickly. "You stupid fellow," she shouted at him. "You've lost the use of your hands again. I told you not to stay out in the sun too long. I hope you're not going to let these two escape. It wouldn't be the first time pilgrims have got away." Then she hurried forward and turned the key firmly in the lock.

"What shall we do?" I whispered to Hopeful, as soon as we were alone. "I'd rather die than be here. Isn't it better to drink the poison than starve to death slowly?"

"I know it's terrible in this place, but the King wouldn't want us to take our own lives," Hopeful said. "If the giant has another fit, he may forget to lock the door. Then we can then slip out before his strength comes back."

Part 1 - Christian's Journey

CHAPTER 32
The Key of Promise

That evening Giant Despair came down to the dungeon again. He was probably hoping to find us both dead, but although we were weak, we were still alive and hadn't touched a drop of the poison.

Giant Despair frightened me so much with his terrible looks and words that I hid in a corner of the dungeon. When at last I looked round, the giant was gone and only Hopeful was with me.

"I think we'll have to take the poison," I said. "I can't bear it here in this stinking place any longer, and we're never going to escape."

"You mustn't talk like that," Hopeful told me confidently. "You're forgetting all the things that have happened since you left the City of Destruction. You weren't afraid to fight the Destroyer, and the King helped you conquer him. You passed safely through the Dark Valley, and even in Vanity Fair the King didn't let the people kill you. Let's trust in him and wait a little longer."

The giant came again later that day, and when he saw we'd still not taken the poison, he told us we would soon wish we'd never been born. When we heard the giant tell his wife about it, she sounded even more angry than her husband.

"Take them into the courtyard tomorrow," she screeched. "Let them see the bones. Then perhaps they'll drink the poison. If they don't, put their eyes out so they'll never be able to see again."

The giant told Diffidence that this sounded like a good plan, and in the morning he dragged us out of the dungeon and led us into the courtyard that was scattered with bones. I had to turn away, and the giant seemed pleased to see how frightened we looked.

"These are the bones of pilgrims," he told us. "They came into my meadow, as you did, and I brought them to my castle. In a few days your bones will lie here in Doubting Castle with the rest."

Then he beat us with his stick, and we lay all day in our dark prison wondering whether our troubles would ever end.

That night, Despair came down with his wife to peer at us through the bars of the dungeon. Hopeful sat with me in the far corner to get as far away from them as possible.

"I just don't understand why they're so brave," Despair said to his wife.

"Perhaps," Diffidence replied, "they think someone is coming to save them. Or maybe they have a key hidden in their clothes to open the doors when we're not watching. You've lost prisoners in that way many times."

Part 1 - Christian's Journey

The giant looked at his wife and grunted. "If they had one of the King's keys, they'd have used it by now. But if it keeps you happy, wife, I'll search them in the morning. Now leave me alone. I'm going upstairs to sleep."

Neither I nor Hopeful could sleep that night, and after talking together for some time, we called to the King's Son, begging him to help us. Of course, we should have done it long ago, but we were too ashamed that we'd taken the wrong path, to ask for help. We were prisoners in Doubting Castle, and I think giant Despair's name had affected us, and so had his wife's, Diffidence. Her name meant Reserved or Timid, and we'd certainly been too timid to approach the King – until now.

"The King's Son will hear us," I said confidently, "even though we can't see him."

I had a sudden thought. It was as though the King's Son was whispering to me, reminding me of something Giant Despair's wife had said.

"Oh, how stupid I've been," I said quietly. "We've stayed here all these days in this dark, stinking dungeon, when we could have got away. When I was leaving the House Beautiful, Discretion gave me a Key called Promise. I remember seeing these words on it: *'I have come as Light into the world, so that everyone who believes in me will not remain in darkness.'* If we tell the King's Son that we're sorry we took the wrong path, I believe this Key will open every one of the giant's locks and take us out of this prison into the light."

We knelt on the filthy floor and begged the King's Son to forgive us for going the wrong way, then reminded him of his promise on the key, knowing it was for us.

Hopeful sprang up. "Let's try it," he said in excitement. "It's not morning yet, and Despair and his wife may still be asleep."

We felt carefully in the darkness until we found the lock of the dungeon door. I pushed the Key of Promise into it, and it turned easily. With our hearts beating fast we stepped over the threshold and listened.

A dim light shone down the passage, and we soon found our way to the gate leading into the courtyard. I slid the Key into the lock, not daring even to whisper.

The Key turned quietly and the gate swung open. I slipped through and Hopeful followed. The moon was shining brightly, and only one more door stood between us and the green meadow.

But this last lock was stiff, and although I tried with all my might, I was unable to turn the Key.

"Oh, *do* try harder," Hopeful cried. "We have to escape before the giant hears us."

"I *am* trying," I insisted, "but the lock's much too stiff."

Hopeful put his hands with mine on the Key of Promise. "I can feel it turning," he said, and in another moment the lock came undone.

We pushed the gate open quickly, but the rusty hinges made such a noise that Giant Despair came running down the stairs. I thought he'd catch us, but just as he reached the

Part 1 - Christian's Journey

doorway his large stick dropped from his hands, and he fell heavily to the ground.

The sun was just coming up over the horizon as we ran towards the stile that led back to the Way of the King.

CHAPTER 33
The Delectable Mountains

We jumped over the stile and sat down by the roadside, still out of breath from running. Somehow, I felt sure Despair wouldn't follow us now we were no longer on his land.

"Well, I'm glad Discretion gave me the Key," I said, as soon as I thought we were safe.

Hopeful agreed. "I don't think we could have escaped without it."

I nodded. "When I held that Key, I thought of all the promises the King's Son has made. But it's a pity pilgrims don't know where that path leads. Maybe we should write a warning on a stone and set it up near the stile."

"We can try," Hopeful suggested. "First, we need to find a stone."

We looked up and down and soon found a large, smooth rock lying in the grass.

"This will do," I said. "You mark out the letters, and then we'll push it into the right place."

Part 1 - Christian's Journey

Hopeful found a large iron nail by the stile, and began to carve some words on the stone. He took some time over his task, but finished it at last.

> *Over this stile is the way to Doubting Castle*
> *Which is kept by Giant Despair,*
> *Who despises the King of the Celestial Country*
> *And seeks to destroy his holy pilgrims.*
> *The Key of Promise opens all the giant's locks.*

We pushed the stone across the grass, and placed it close to the stile so that no one could pass by without seeing it.

"It will be sure to save someone," Hopeful said. "I'm glad you thought of it."

As we walked on, slowly and painfully, we came to a place where a range of hills rose in front of us.

Hopeful pointed ahead. "I wonder what the view is like from the top. It looks as though the Way of the King goes right over these hills."

The hills looked familiar, and then I realized why. "I saw them in the distance when I was at the House Beautiful," I told Hopeful, "but I can't remember what they're called. I think there are some shepherds there who help pilgrims."

As we came close to the mountains, we found gardens and orchards, and vineyards and fountains of water, so we took the opportunity to wash ourselves clean of the filth and smell from the giant's dungeon. Then we ate some of the fruit and drank clear, fresh water from a spring.

The shepherds weren't far above the path, and four of them hurried down to greet us. "Welcome to the Delectable Mountains," they said. "This country is called Immanuel's Land. It belongs to the King's Son, and you can sometimes see the King's City from the top of these hills."

"Are these his sheep," I asked, pointing to the flock they were looking after.

"These sheep are here as a picture of the Celestial City, for pilgrims to see," one shepherd said. "The King's Son has rescued each of these sheep from danger, just as he rescued you. Now he is making sure they are cared for in safety."

"Is it far to the Celestial City?" I asked.

"And is the way safe?" Hopeful added.

The shepherd scratched his chin. "It's safe for those who love the King, but pilgrims who don't serve him faithfully can fall into danger."

"We're both tired. Is there anywhere for pilgrims to rest?" I asked.

"Of course there is," the shepherd replied. "The King wants us to do everything we can to help his servants as they pass over these mountains. Come with us, and we'll take good care of you."

The shepherds introduced themselves as Knowledge, Experience, Watchful, and Sincere, and led us to their tents where they gave us plenty of good, nourishing food.

"I can see how exhausted you are," Watchful said after the meal. "It's late, and I think it's time you were both in bed."

Part 1 - Christian's Journey

So the two of us slept comfortably, and I woke early in the morning feeling much less sore after my beating in Doubting Castle. I hoped that one day some pilgrims would come here and kill Giant Despair and his wife, and destroy their home. I certainly hoped they would.

CHAPTER 34
Mount Caution

The next morning the shepherds asked us if we'd like to see some of the special sights on the mountains before we left. I thought this sounded good, so they led us up the first hill.

We soon came to a steep and rugged path that was hard to climb. It led to the top of a large rock on the edge of the hill, and when we looked down, we could see a valley far below.

"Do pilgrims ever fall over here?" Hopeful asked.

"Sometimes," the shepherds replied. "This is the Rock of Error. It's dangerous for pilgrims to climb onto this Rock without a guide."

"Why would anyone try to do that?" I asked.

"Because they think they'll have a better view," the shepherd called Experience explained. "But when they look over, the sight of the deep valley makes them unsteady and occasionally they fall."

Then the shepherds took us to another place, called Mount Caution. From it we could see people shuffling along in the

Part 1 - Christian's Journey

valley far below, reaching out their hands as if to feel what was in front. I noticed that they kept bumping into rocks.

"Are they blind?" I asked.

Watchful told me they were. "Did you see a stile leading to By-Path Meadow, not far from here?" he asked.

I nodded.

"Well, over that stile there's a path to a castle where Giant Despair lives. Just before you get there, the Way of the King is rough and stony, and the giant's path in the meadow is soft and green. It looks safe, but it's a dangerous path to take."

"We found it," Hopeful said quietly. "And we used it."

Watchful nodded. "Then you'll know that if pilgrims take the easy path, Despair catches them and carries them to his prison in Doubting Castle. He beats them and sometimes makes them blind. Then he brings them down here, where they wander about unable to go on with their journey."

Hopeful looked at me, but said nothing. I realized that if we hadn't escaped from Doubting Castle, with the help of the Key of Promise, we might be down there now, stumbling into the rocks.

The shepherds started down the hill, on the side farthest from the Way of the King. We soon came to a spot that reminded me of the entrance to the Dark Valley. Huge black rocks rose high above the path on both sides, and we could only see a little distance down the narrow road because of a thick mist.

"This is another dangerous place," Knowledge explained, holding us back firmly. "From time to time pilgrims who walk over the mountains get lost here. That dark path leads into the country of the evil prince, and it can take pilgrims a long time to find their way out – if they find it at all."

Part 1 - Christian's Journey

CHAPTER 35
Ignorance

As we reached the last of the hills, the shepherds told us it was called Mount Clear. We climbed to the top to look ahead, for the day was bright. A light shone in the far distance, dazzling my eyes.

"Do you see that light?" the shepherd called Sincere asked us. "That's the Celestial City. If your eyes are good you may be able to see its Gates."

But the light was brighter than the sun at midday, and the glory of that City was too great for human eyes to bear.

"I can only see something shining," I said, screwing up my eyes.

"It certainly is too bright for you," Sincere told me, "but we have a telescope called Faith, which will make it seem clearer."

I took the telescope, but the thought of the dangers we had just seen made me tremble, and my hands shook so much that I was unable to hold it steady.

Then Hopeful tried. "I think I can see something like large gates made of gold."

Experience let us both look for some time before taking the telescope back from us. He said it was time for us to continue our journey. "But before you leave," he added, "I have a warning to give you. When you have traveled a little further, you may meet a man called the Flatterer. He will try to lead you out of the Way of the King by praising you, and saying wonderful things about you, but you must not listen to him."

Watchful then explained that we were close to a place called the Enchanted Ground, where the air made all pilgrims sleepy. "It's part of the evil prince's country. If his servants find you sleeping there, they'll try to carry you away," he warned us.

"We'll give you this map," Knowledge added, putting a sheet of paper into my hand. "All the places you have to pass through are marked on it, and if you look at it carefully you'll not lose your way."

I folded it up, tucked it into a pocket and forgot about it. As I walked out down the mountain path with Hopeful, we talked together about everything the shepherds had shown us.

"If I could only have seen the Celestial City," I said. "I really wanted to see it."

"Well," Hopeful replied, "I'm sure I saw the Gates, and we know it's not far away now."

At the foot of the mountain we came to a twisting lane leading off the Way of the King. The signpost said the lane led to a place called Conceit, and a boy was running from there towards us.

"What sort of place is Conceit?" I asked him.

Part 1 - Christian's Journey

"It's a large town where I live, beyond the hills," the boy replied. "My name is Ignorance, and I've decided to go to the Celestial City."

"Do you think they'll let you in?" I asked in surprise, wondering why he had come from the wrong direction.

"Why not? They let everybody in."

I shook my head. "We have our Rolls of Faith to show that our names are already written in the Celestial City. Did the King give you anything?"

"No, but I can't see it will matter. I've lived a good life and always tried to help people. I even call to the King sometimes. *You* can follow the King in whatever way you like, and *I'll* follow him my way. All right? You have *your* faith and I have *mine*. I expect mine is just as good as yours."

"But," I said, "the King's pilgrims have to be welcomed in by his Son at the Wicket Gate, and go past the Cross. The King's Son says he is the only Way to start. Did you do that?"

"You needn't make such a fuss about it," Ignorance snapped. "I don't know where you've come from, but you were probably living near the Wicket Gate, so of course it was easy for you. Nobody in the town of Conceit *ever* thinks of starting there. In fact, I don't believe anybody knows this Wicket Gate you're talking about. We have a gentle pathway that saves us such a lot of trouble, and of course it makes our pilgrimage shorter."

I didn't know what to say, and as Ignorance stopped to gather some fruit, Hopeful looked at me and we moved off without him.

When Ignorance didn't run after us, Hopeful said, "Should we wait?"

"Ignorance isn't stupid," I said, "but he's unaware of his dangerous position. He has a false faith in his own good behavior, and refuses to believe differently. If he wants to know about the Way to the King, he'll soon catch us up. I'd like to help him if we can, but we mustn't let him stop us going."

Part 1 - Christian's Journey

CHAPTER 36
Little-Faith

We were just passing a track called Dead Man's Lane, when we saw a band of soldiers in the distance. They were clothed in dark armor that didn't shine like mine, and we guessed straight away that they belonged to the army of the evil prince.

"Do you think they'll hurt us?" Hopeful asked.

"I don't know," I said, "but we won't wait around to see."

So although we both felt frightened, we kept steadily on our way. As the soldiers drew near, I saw they had a prisoner with them, and I could see by his clothes he was one of the King's pilgrims. The soldiers stopped for a rest, although they took no notice of us.

The pilgrim hung down his head, as though ashamed to let us see his face. "My name is Turn-Away," he said quietly. "I loved the King once. I almost reached the Gates of the Celestial City, but one day I wandered from the straight path and met some servants of the evil prince who pretended to be kind to me."

"What happened?" I whispered, for I could see the soldiers looking at us.

"Well," the prisoner said, "I stayed with them, and of course I soon forgot the good King. I let my armor grow rusty, and my new clothes became dirty and ragged. I lost my Roll of Faith, and no one would ever have known I'd once served the King."

"Why are you a prisoner?" I asked, more loudly now, for the soldiers were no longer taking any notice.

"One day something reminded me of the Celestial City, and I began to feel sorry and wondered whether the King would forgive me. So I left my new friends and tried to find my way back to the straight path. The evil prince heard I'd gone, and sent these soldiers to look for me. I tried to defend myself with my sword, but it was too rusty to use. So here I am, bound with chains, and they're taking me back to the country of the evil prince."

At that moment the soldiers moved off, taking their prisoner with them. I was glad that the soldiers hadn't spoken to us, but I felt sorry for the pilgrim who seemed to be in great trouble.

"We must ask the King to rescue him," I said, and we fell to our knees and begged the King to send someone to release Turn-Away from the power of the evil prince.

"When I was at the House Beautiful, I read a story of a young pilgrim named Little-Faith from the town of Sincere," I said. "He was robbed not far from here, at the corner of Dead

Man's Lane. I think the evil prince's servants come looking for pilgrims who are lazy, so we'll have to be careful."

"Tell me about Little-Faith," Hopeful said. "How was he robbed?"

"He was tired," I explained, "and he sat down on the grass to rest. Three brothers – I think their names were Faint-Heart, Mistrust and Guilt – were walking down Dead Man's Lane. They saw Little-Faith on the grass fast asleep, so thought they'd steal his things. Before Little-Faith had time to wake up and get his sword, they beat him dreadfully. They took all the money out of his pockets, and then they thought they heard someone coming."

"Who was it?"

"There wasn't anyone really, but they knew they were doing wrong and they were frightened. There's a village called Good Confidence somewhere in these mountains, and one of the King's servants, Captain Great-Grace, lives there. The boys thought he was coming, so they ran away."

"And what happened to Little-Faith? Did he go on with his journey"

"He did, but he was always poor, because the three brothers had stolen his money. But they didn't take the precious things the King had given him. So although he was badly injured and had lost his money, he realized things could have been worse. But he was always short of food."

"He could have sold some of the things the King gave him," Hopeful said.

I shook my head. "The King's gifts are too precious to sell," I told him. "Everything the King gives us is given for a good reason."

CHAPTER 37
Caught in the Net

We were still talking about Little-Faith and his troubles, when we came to a place where the road divided into two. I looked back and saw that Ignorance was following, but every time we stopped, he stopped. Clearly, he had no intention of walking with us.

Ahead of us was a problem. Instead of one way being straight and narrow, and the other wide and going in the wrong direction, I couldn't decide which path was the right one. When I stood with Hopeful on one side of the road, the right-hand path seemed to be narrow as well as straight. But when we crossed over, the left-hand path looked the same.

"I don't know *which* is right," I said.

We spent a long time crossing the road from side to side, trying to work out which was the straighter of the two paths. Presently a man came up behind us. His face looked hard and unkind, but because he wore a white robe we thought he must be a pilgrim.

"Whatever's the matter?" he asked. "You look puzzled."

"Oh," I said, "we're going to the King's City, and we can't make out which of these paths is the one to take."

The man laughed. "Is that all? I'm going to the Celestial City myself. Follow me and I'll show you the way. What clever, sensible young pilgrims you must be, to be taking so much care to find the right path."

So we followed him. But instead of going towards the Celestial City, the path started to turn, more and more, until I realized we going back towards the Delectable Mountains.

"*This* path isn't the right one," I whispered to Hopeful.

Hopeful stopped at once. "Don't you think so?" he asked quietly.

I shook my head. "There are the Delectable Mountains, where we were this morning with the shepherds."

"What are we going to do?" Hopeful asked in alarm.

The answer was obvious. "We must go back."

At that moment the man turned. Before we had time to take another step, he flung a large net over us.

We fell to the ground, trapped and shouting for help, but the man only laughed as he walked away. As he went out of sight his white robe slipped from his shoulders, and I realized he was a servant of the evil prince who had dressed himself like a pilgrim, to deceive anyone who would listen to him.

We struggled hard to free ourselves, but the more we pulled at it, the tighter the net got. At last we lay still, wondering how we could have been so stupid.

"Do you think he was the Flatterer?" I said. "The shepherds *told* us not to listen to him."

Hopeful shook his head sadly. "And we never even looked at the map they gave us. If we had, we'd have known this is the wrong path."

"We're not good pilgrims," I said. "We've gone the wrong way so many times. If only the King will save us just this once, I promise I'll never do anything wrong again."

CHAPTER 38
Rescue

"We're not going to get out," Hopeful said, trying once again to untangle us from the heavy net. "Where's that man gone?"

"Perhaps he's gone to tell the evil prince about us," I said. "Then he'll send his soldiers to carry us off – like Turn-Away."

Then, just when the sun was setting, we heard footsteps getting closer. I could feel Hopeful tremble, but only one man came in sight. I knew by his shining garments and gentle face he was one of the King's servants.

When he saw us, he stopped. "How did you get into this net?" he asked.

I took a deep breath. "We couldn't decide which road to take. Then a man with a white robe came up to us and told us he was going to the Celestial City, so we followed him."

"It was the Flatterer," the man told us, confirming our own suspicion. Then he stooped down and tore a large hole in the net.

We were soon able to crawl out of it, and stood on the path before him, waiting for him to tell us what to do. His face

Part 1 - Christian's Journey

seemed serious, and I remembered how Evangelist had looked at me in the same way, when he found me wandering amongst the terrifying rocks on Mount Law before I reached the Wicket Gate.

The King's servant turned towards the Way of the King, and told us to come after him. When we were once more in the right path, he stopped. "Where did you sleep last night?" he asked.

"On the Delectable Mountains with the shepherds," I said.

"Then where is your map of the Way?"

We hung down our heads, for we felt ashamed.

"Did you look at your map when you were unsure which way to go?"

"No," Hopeful whispered.

I added, "I forgot we had it."

"And what else did the shepherds say to you? Did they warn you about the Flatterer?"

"They told us not to listen to him."

"And yet you *did* listen. How was that?"

I looked at the ground. "He told us we were such clever and sensible pilgrims to be taking so much care to find the right path. I didn't think that man *could* be the Flatterer, he was so friendly."

The man laid his hands on our shoulders, and spoke gently. "You have been foolish," he said, "but I think you're sorry."

"We *are* sorry," I insisted, "and it was more my fault than Hopeful's."

"No," the King's servant said, "you were *both* wrong. If the King had not sent me to look for you, you might have been carried away by the soldiers of the evil prince."

"We're so thankful that you came," Hopeful said.

"I am glad to hear it," the man told him. "But although the King sends me to seek for lost pilgrims and to bring them back to the right path, he is not pleased with you, although he loves you so much."

"Will he forgive us?" I asked anxiously. "I've promised never to do anything wrong again."

"The King has already forgiven you," the King's servant said. "You may intend to keep your promise, but you will keep making mistakes on your journey. The King understands, and will forgive you every time you ask. You have been pilgrims for a long time now, and should have known better than to go your own way. So I hope you have learnt a lesson from all this."

"I know we have," I said. "It's not always easy to go the right way. Are you sure the King understands how difficult it is for us?"

"The King's Son was once a pilgrim himself," the servant told us. "He has not forgotten the dangers and difficulties of the Way."

Part 1 - Christian's Journey

CHAPTER 39
Unbelief

After the King's servant left, we continued on the right path, when suddenly Hopeful held me by the arm. "See that man? I think he wants to talk to us."

The man was walking towards us, away from the Celestial City.

Hopeful sounded puzzled. "He's wearing pilgrim's clothes, so why is he walking the wrong way?"

The man stopped and asked where we were going. He said his name was Atheist, but added that everyone called him Unbelief. I thought he had a pleasant face, and his voice sounded gentle, but I felt we'd be wise not to trust him. We'd just had a bad experience with the Flatterer, who also said nice things.

"We're going to the Celestial City, the City of the King," was all I said.

Unbelief started to laugh loudly.

"Why are you laughing?" I asked.

"I'm laughing because you're both so stupid," Unbelief said. "Have you really traveled all this way without discovering the truth?"

"Do you think we won't be received when we arrive?" Hopeful asked.

"Received?" Unbelief said. "There's no such place as you dream of in all this world."

"But there is in the world to come," I said.

"Oh, you poor pilgrims," Unbelief said, still laughing. "I've been looking for the Celestial City for twenty years, and I'm no nearer finding it than I was on the first day I set out."

"You're wrong," I said. "Not only have we heard about it, but we're going there."

"You're going nowhere." Unbelief had an unpleasant smile now. "Oh yes, I once thought as you do, but now I'm going home and intend to forget all about my foolishness."

I turned to Hopeful. "Do you trust him?" I asked quietly.

"No," Hopeful said, "I don't."

"And neither do I," I said firmly, remembering the view we had from the Delectable Mountains. "Come on, Hopeful, let's keep going or we'll miss the path again."

Unbelief stood watching. "Come with me," he offered, "and I'll take you safely back to your homes. Your friends will be glad to see you."

I shook my head firmly. "You're trying to deceive us, but we don't believe anything you say. The King's word is true. There *is* a Celestial City. We saw its light when we were with the shepherds."

Unbelief shook his head. "You're mistaken, but go and look for it if you want to. I'm going back to my own country."

"And *we* are going to the King," I replied.

So we went on again, and Unbelief carried on laughing as he turned away.

CHAPTER 40
The Enchanted Ground

At last we came to a wide plain, between the Delectable Mountains and a country with low hills and long valleys. We looked at our map and saw that this was called the Enchanted Ground.

Hopeful yawned, and said, "I'm too tired to go on. Let's lie down and rest."

I thought he sounded ready for sleep. "Not here," I said quickly.

"Why not?" Hopeful asked drowsily. "There's no one to hurt us. You go on. I'll only be a few minutes."

He lay down on the grass, but I quickly pulled him up and shook him hard. "What *are* you thinking about, Hopeful? Don't you remember the shepherds warned us about the Enchanted Ground? They told us not to sleep here."

Hopeful seemed suddenly wide awake. "Sorry," he said, "but I don't think I've ever felt so sleepy before. Imagine what would have happened if I'd been here alone. I might never have

Part 1 - Christian's Journey

woken up. We've come a long way, and I don't want to be carried off like Turn-Away."

"I'm feeling sleepy, too," I admitted. "Let's talk about something interesting. That will keep us awake. You've never told me how you began to be a pilgrim."

"I started out before you did," Hopeful told me. "I knew Evangelist well, and he used to tell me about the King. I was living a dishonest sort of life, but I shut my eyes and ears to anything to do with the King and his Son. Then, one day, I decided to do something about it."

"What?" I asked.

"I decided to make my own changes," Hopeful said, as we walked quickly. "I stopped doing and saying bad things, called to the King a bit and that sort of thing."

"You were a bit like Ignorance," I say.

Hopeful nodded. "Perhaps I was. But the changes didn't make any difference. I knew that inside I was as bad as ever."

"Tell me more," I urged.

Hopeful smiled in embarrassment. "Every time I heard anyone mention the King and his Son, or I heard about someone going to the Celestial City, I thought it was time to start working my way there. But Evangelist told me it was no good trying to get there by pleasing the King. I had to start at the Wicket Gate and go to the Cross – just as I was. So I ran there and began my journey the proper way. But when I came to Vanity Fair I felt tired, and the people persuaded me not to go any further. I liked it there, so I stayed."

This surprised me, for I'd found the town unpleasant. "You really liked Vanity Fair?"

"Well, I liked it sometimes, but I often felt frightened and unhappy. When pilgrims passed through the town, I was afraid they'd recognize me. Then you came with Faithful, and the minute I saw you I felt so ashamed of my life."

"Did you see us being beaten?" I asked.

"Yes, and I watched you when you were in the cage. Once I crept up close to the bars. I think you must have been asleep, but Faithful saw me and spoke to me."

"What did he say?"

"He begged me to leave the city at once, and told me the King's Son loves me and would forgive me if I told him I was sorry. I can remember some words he told me, words that were spoken by the King's Son. 'I will never turn away anyone who comes to me.' Then I saw Faithful killed because he loved the King, and I made up my mind that if you were set free, I'd ask you to let me go with you."

"I'm glad you did," I said.

Hopeful nodded. "I'm glad too, Christian. Glad the King's Son hasn't turned me away, and glad to know he never will."

Part 1 - Christian's Journey

CHAPTER 41
Ignorance Again

Ignorance had been following us off and on for some time, and when Hopeful looked back he told me he could see him again. "He's only a little way behind us," Hopeful said. "How has he been so quick? Didn't the Flatter and Unbelief try to stop him?"

"I don't expect they took any notice of him," I said. "He didn't start in the right place, and they know that when he reaches the Celestial City he won't be allowed inside."

"Shall we wait for him?" Hopeful asked.

"Perhaps it would be better," I said. "If he feels sleepy we can at least keep him awake."

We waited, but although Ignorance must have seen us waiting, he took a long time to catch up.

"It's is a pity for you to stay behind," I said to Ignorance, as he sauntered slowly towards us. "Come and walk with us. We can help you start your journey the right way."

Ignorance shrugged. "I'd just as soon walk by myself. I always have so much to think about."

"What do you think about?" Hopeful asked.

"About the King and the Celestial City."

"But *thinking* about them isn't enough," I told him. "The evil prince thinks about them, too – but he's not allowed in."

I noticed Ignorance turning red with anger. "I suppose you think you're so perfect," he snapped.

"No, I don't," I said. "The King's Son is the one who's perfect, and he's promised us a place."

"Perhaps he's promised one to me," Ignorance said.

"Ask him if he has," I suggested.

Ignorance shook his head. "That sort of thing is all too much trouble, if you want to know."

"We can only get into the City if we've been forgiven," I told him. "No one gets in just by being good."

"We'll see about that." Ignorance sat down angrily on the grass. "I've left my home, and now I'm living like a pilgrim. What else can I do? Anyone would think I wasn't already good enough to be a pilgrim."

"We can never make ourselves good enough for the King," I said. "That's why his Son agreed to die on the Cross, to save us from punishment. There's a rhyme I know:

"The King was angry with us all,
'I'll punish you,' he said;
But then he took his only Son
And punished him instead."

Part 1 - Christian's Journey

Ignorance just shrugged, as though it didn't matter to him one way or the other.

I turn to Hopeful. "I don't know what else to say," I whispered. "No one is good enough to get into the Celestial City by themselves, but Ignorance won't believe us."

Ignorance seemed to be tired of talking. "You two have such silly ideas," he sighed. "I don't want to walk with you anymore."

"Come on, Hopeful," I said, "it looks as though we'll be traveling by ourselves again."

As we went ahead, Hopeful shook his head in wonder. "If everyone gets to the Celestial City, why did we have to pass by the Cross and go through all those difficulties?" he asked.

"We'll watch and see what happens to Ignorance at the Dark River," I said. "I think you'll get your answer then."

CHAPTER 42
The Land of Beulah

"I hope we're almost past the Enchanted Ground," Hopeful said, yawning loudly.

"Are you tired?" I asked.

Hopeful sighed. "A bit. Perhaps we've been talking too much."

I took out the shepherds' map. "We're close to the Land of Beulah."

Hopeful looked brighter when he heard that. "Come on," he said, speeding up, "I can't wait to get there."

It seemed only a few minutes before we left the Enchanted Ground and entered the country of Beulah. The air was sweet and pleasant, and I was pleased to see from my map that the Way of the King led right through it.

I couldn't remember ever seeing so many flowers, and hearing so many different birds sing. The sun shone all the time, for we were now past the Dark Valley, out of the reach of Giant Despair, and we certainly couldn't see places like Doubting Castle and Vanity Fair from here.

Part 1 - Christian's Journey

What we could see was the Celestial City across the Dark River. As I looked at it, and knew the City was where the King and his Son lived, I began to feel unsteady with joy. As I sat down to recover, Hopeful sat with me.

"The thought of what's ahead after our journey is almost too much to take in," he said, as his eyes sparkled.

As soon as we were feeling better, we continued on our way, going past orchards, vineyards and gardens. Although they were fenced in, there were open gates to go through.

I saw a man standing, watching us. We told him who we were and he explained he was the gardener.

"Who do all these gardens and orchards belong to?" I asked.

"They are the King's," he said. "He planted them here for his own enjoyment, and also as a place where pilgrims like you can rest."

The gardener then invited us to pick fruit and refresh ourselves. "There is a shelter here, where you can sleep," he said, showing us an arbor built from timber and green leaves.

* * *

"Oh, Hopeful," I said one evening, as we sat watching the sun slowly disappear behind the hills, "aren't you glad we came? I seem to be forgetting all the troubles we've had, now that we're happy."

"I'm ever so pleased I ran away from Vanity Fair," Hopeful told me, clapping his hands in joy. "And I'm glad I didn't lose my Roll of Faith there. I don't know how I managed to keep it safely. The King's Son must surely have been helping me."

The gardener came up and stood with us. "Do you know you both talk in your sleep?" he said, with a smile.

I had no idea. "What do we say?" I asked, afraid I might have said things that would displease the King.

"You say only good things," the gardener explained, perhaps reading my thoughts. "Your heads are so full of the King and his Son that even when you are asleep you have to talk about them."

I rather liked the thought of that. "What happens to pilgrims now?" I asked.

The man sat down with us and put a hand on his chin, deep in thought. "Some pilgrims live quietly in this land for many years," he said, "but often the King gives them work to do in the country of the evil prince, before they go to the Celestial City to live with him forever."

"I can remember when Help pulled me out of the Slough of Despond," I told the gardener. "He said he'd been to the Gates of the City, but the King had given him some work to do before he could enter it. I'll go away and work for the King if he wants me to, but I think I'd like best to go straight to the City."

"So would I," Hopeful agreed.

The King's gardener was quick to tell us of the good things that lay ahead. So we stayed happily in Beulah, talking and thinking about the King. A few angels walked with us from time to time, for we were on the border of the Celestial City.

Part 1 - Christian's Journey

CHAPTER 43
Ignorance at the River

We watched Ignorance walk past the gates of the King's gardens, but he wasn't wearing the King's clothes, and the gardener didn't invite him in. I noticed that the angels, although they saw Ignorance as he walked along, didn't speak to him or give him any encouraging messages from the King.

One day we followed Ignorance to the bank of the Dark River. He kept looking across at the walls of the Celestial City, then he stepped into the water. The water was rough today, and he jumped back out with a puzzled look on his face.

"I don't want to cross just yet," I heard him say.

I hurried over to him. "It's still not too late to go through the Wicket Gate and find the Cross," I said. "I can show you the Way."

Ignorance shook his head. "I can't be bothered about that sort of thing now. Anyway, it's probably too late."

"No, it's never too late," I insisted. "Not until you cross the Dark River. I know the Way, and I can take you there if you like."

Ignorance sighed. "That's where I'm going." He pointed to the walls of the Celestial City. "I've not been a bad person, so I don't think there'll be any problems. Anyway, someone else will be crossing soon, and I can see how they get on. I can't see a bridge, so maybe there's a boat to carry the pilgrims over."

"There *is* a boat," a voice said behind us.

We turned quickly to see who was speaking. It was the King's gardener.

"There *is* a boat," he repeated quietly, out of the hearing of Ignorance, "but it belongs to the evil prince, and the King's pilgrims never use it. The boatman's name is Vain-Hope. Here he comes now. Look, he's seen Ignorance sitting on the grass and he's rowing towards him."

"Come on, Ignorance, it's time for you to cross over," the boatman called, as he drew his craft into the riverbank. "I've brought my boat for you."

Ignorance looked pleased and got up at once, saying, "I suppose the King sent you."

"Of course," Vain-Hope replied, but it sounded like a lie. "The water isn't as deep as it looks, and many pilgrims try to walk through it. But there's no need for you to do that, because I'm ready to take you over."

He held out his hand and Ignorance took it, stepping into the boat. Then Vain-Hope picked up his oars and prepared to row across the rough water.

"What do I do when I get to the other side," we heard Ignorance ask.

Vain-Hope pointed to a path on the opposite bank. "That's the best way," he explained. "It's smooth and easy. If the King's angels had come to meet you, they'd have taken you by another road that's steep and difficult to climb. Go straight up to the Gates, and you'll soon find your way to the King's palace."

We watched the boat reach the far bank of the River where Ignorance got out. He turned round and began to climb the path towards the City.

"What will happen to him now?" I asked the gardener.

"Ignorance will come to a gateway," the gardener said. "On the archway he will see some words written in large letters:

> BLESSED ARE THOSE WHO WASH THEIR ROBES,
> THEY WILL HAVE THE RIGHT
> TO EAT FROM THE TREE OF LIFE,
> AND GO THROUGH THE GATES
> INTO THE CITY."

"Will Ignorance go in?" Hopeful asked.

The gardener shook his head. "Ignorance will think to himself that he's tried to do his best, so he'll call out, 'I am a pilgrim, and I have just crossed the River. I wish to live in the Celestial City.'"

I frowned. "And then?"

The gardener looked unhappy. "Then Ignorance will be asked for his Roll of Faith. I have seen it happen many times. He will put his hand into his pockets and pretend to feel for it."

"Won't he be let in?" Hopeful asked.

"The City is so beautiful," I added. "I want to live there forever."

"And so you will," the gardener assured us. "You came through the Wicket Gate and went past the Cross. The King's own Son built the Wicket Gate, but Ignorance chose not to go through it. So he has no place in the Celestial City."

Part 1 - Christian's Journey

CHAPTER 44
"Do Not Be Afraid."

After Ignorance had crossed the Dark River, I often sat with Hopeful to watch angels from the Celestial City come across to visit the people who lived with us in the land of Beulah. Sometimes they brought messages from the King to his servants, and we learnt that it would not be long before a message was given to us.

One morning, when we were walking slowly among the vines, we saw two angels coming down the path to meet us.

"Are you traveling to the Celestial City?" the angels said.

"Yes," we replied together.

The angels asked us many questions, and we told them everything that had happened since we began our pilgrimage. I told of my difficulties and dangers, and Hopeful explained how he'd wasted so much time in Vanity Fair.

"We've often behaved badly," I said, "but we've been sorry afterwards."

"We have," Hopeful added quietly.

"Forgiveness is a gift offered by the King, and you have accepted it," the angels told us.

"And we love the King with all our hearts," I said.

"He knows you do," the angels replied. "He's sent us to tell you he wants you to enter his City."

When Hopeful heard this, he said he felt excited. I wanted to feel like that, but when I thought of meeting the King I became anxious, and said to the angels, "Will you go with us?"

"We will go with you a little way," they said, "and meet you again at the Gates of the Celestial City."

They asked us to follow them, and we went out of the garden and down to the edge of the Dark River. The reflection of the sun shining on the other side was so glorious today that I wasn't able to see across, but the water between us and the Celestial City looked especially deep.

"Oh," I cried, almost in panic, "if we don't use Vain-Hope's boat, how are we to get there?"

"You have to walk through the water," the angels replied, "but there is no need to be afraid. The King's City is on the other side, and you will soon be safely inside its Gates."

Hopeful raised his head and looked across the river. "Look," he said, "I can see the Golden Gates. Oh, Christian, why are you frightened?"

"It's all right for you," I said in despair, "but the King is never going to receive me. I've been a bad pilgrim."

I could no longer see the light beyond the Dark River, and I shivered as I looked into the cold water, then turned once more to the angels. "It's too deep," I said. "I'll be drowned."

Part 1 - Christian's Journey

"No," the angels told me, "you won't find it too deep. Don't look at the water, Christian, but lift up your eyes to the light, and the King will help you."

I tried to be brave. "Do the King's pilgrims always cross safely?"

"Yes, Christian, always," the angels said. "Do not be afraid. Trust in the King, and remember all that he has done for you through his Son."

Then the angels turned away, and Hopeful put his arm round my shoulders. "Come on, Christian, we'll soon be over. I know the King will take care of us."

Then we walked slowly down the bank and stepped into the cold River.

CHAPTER 45
The Celestial City

I felt the water pulling at me, trying to drag me under. But Hopeful held me tightly, his eyes fixed on the far bank.

"I keep thinking of all the bad things I've done in my life," I gasped, as a wave hit me in the face. "You go on, Hopeful. I don't deserve to get safely across."

Hopeful wasn't giving up on me. "I can see people waiting for us on the other side," he said. "Just keep going. The King loves you and wants you with him."

As soon as Hopeful said this, I could hear the King's Son calling to me with words I'd read in my Book. "When you pass through the waters, I will be with you."

Then I found my courage returning, and I could touch the bed of the river with my feet and walk to the far bank. The two angels who had led us down to the Dark River were there to receive us. They said, "Come, we will take you to the Gates of the City."

The City stood on a great hill, but we went up to it easily because the angels held us by our arms. I looked down at my

Part 1 - Christian's Journey

clothes, wondering if I'd kept them clean enough to meet the King and his Son. To my amazement I saw we'd been given shining clothes, and far below, floating away in the River, were the ones we'd traveled in.

Suddenly we were swept up by a host of angels telling us about the beauty and joy that we would find in the Holy City.

"You are going to the City of the King," they said. "You will find the tree of life, and eat of its never-fading fruits. You will be able to walk and talk every day with the King in your new clothes, even all the days of eternity."

I looked at Hopeful. "I want to thank the King and his Son for bringing us safely here," I said, in tears.

"And so you shall," the angels said. "The King's Son will wipe away every tear from your eyes. There will no longer be any death. There will no longer be any mourning, or crying or pain. All that is in the past."

"And what are we to do now?" I asked.

The angels smiled. "You will be able to praise the King with shouting and thanksgiving. You tried to serve him in the world, but here in the Celestial City you will be able to do it with a freedom you never knew before. You will meet your family and friends who have already crossed the Dark River, and they will welcome you with joy."

We came to an archway, over which were written the words the gardener had told us about:

BLESSED ARE THOSE WHO WASH THEIR ROBES,
THEY WILL HAVE THE RIGHT
TO EAT FROM THE TREE OF LIFE,
AND GO THROUGH THE GATES
INTO THE CITY

The King's servant looked down from the archway and took our Rolls of Faith to carry to the King. The Rolls were sealed with the King's Son's own seal, and I knew that when the King saw the seal he would be glad.

Sure enough, the servant returned quickly and ordered the Gates to be opened, so he could take us to the King.

The people of the Celestial City heard the sound of the silver trumpets, and knew what it meant. When we passed through the gateway, we found young Faithful and my mother, and a great crowd waiting to receive us with music and songs of welcome. I noticed that Hopeful didn't have any friends to greet him, for he'd left them behind in the City of Destruction. But people gathered round and spoke kindly to him, and he seemed to forget his loneliness immediately.

Then I heard the bells in the City ring again for joy, and the King's Son came to us, and said, "You are good and faithful servants. Come and share my joy."

The City shone like the sun, and the streets were paved with gold. People walked with crowns on their heads, palms in their hands, and golden harps to sing praises.

Then Hopeful sang with me, "Blessing and honor and glory and power belong to the One sitting on the throne, and to the Lamb forever and ever."

I knew then that the King's Son was the Lamb. He had sacrificed himself, taking away all my guilt and wrongdoing, so I could stand here in front of him, washed clean.

Then the King's Son held me securely in his arms. "Do not be afraid, Christian" he said. "I am the First and the Last. I am the Living One. I was dead, but now I am alive for ever and ever."

And the angels sang, "Holy, holy, holy is the Lord God Almighty."

I was in Heaven!

Chris Wright

PART 2

CHRISTIANA'S STORY

Part 2 - Christiana's Story

CHAPTER 1
The Letter

MY NAME IS CHRISTIANA. I live in a place called the City of Destruction, which is as bad a city to live in as its name suggests. The only place where I feel happy is on the hill above the city, which is where I am now. Far below, people are going about their work. I like to sit up high like this, where I once sat with my friend Christian – before he went on his journey. I have my four brothers with me today, and they're all younger than me. I'm fourteen, and I'm worried how I'm going to look after my brothers in the coming winter.

I often think about the journey Christian made, and wonder where he's living. Is he in the Celestial City? That's what some people call it. Did he reach it, or was he lost crossing the Dark River?

The Celestial City. Even the name sounds good, so what must it be like to live there? While my mother and father were traveling to the Celestial City, along the Way of the King, they begged me to start my journey soon – and take my brothers with me. Last year my father entered the Dark River. A few days later, my mother followed him.

Christian often talked about a special Book he was reading, but I didn't really believe what the Book said. "If my father and mother are living in a beautiful place," I once told him, "they'd have sent me a message. I think I'll never see them again."

I look across the open fields and can see a light shining brightly in the distance. I remember Christian telling me there's a high wall there, and a large door in it with a Wicket Gate where pilgrims must start their journey.

Perhaps we'll all go there one day. Matthew and Samuel are probably old enough to go with me now, but as I look at Joseph and James they seem rather young. I think I'll have to wait, because I can't leave them behind. I stand up and signal to my four brothers to follow me back to our home in the City of Destruction.

* * *

It's the evening now, and I've prepared tea for my brothers, which went down well. The four boys are out in the streets with their friends, and the house is quiet. I sit by the fire and keep thinking about our father and mother – and about Christian.

In the night I have a lovely dream. I'm in the Celestial City, walking along its streets with Christian. My brothers are there with us. We go into a wonderful palace where the King's Son meets us and speaks to us.

I wake up with a jump. I wish it had been true, and not just a dream. I try to get back to sleep to continue dreaming, but it's no good. So although it's early, I get dressed and begin to tidy

Part 2 - Christiana's Story

the house. After breakfast, I jump as someone knocks on the door, and I open it cautiously to see who's calling.

I expect to see a neighbor, but a woman visiting the city is standing there. She says her name is Wisdom, and she's the daughter of Evangelist. I remember seeing Evangelist in the city, and sometimes I've even stopped to listen as he tells us about the King.

"Christiana, I've wanted to speak to you for some time," Wisdom says, "but I've not been able to find you in the streets."

"No," I say, "I'm tired of the city, so I usually go up the hill to get away from it."

Wisdom lays her hand on my shoulder. "I don't think you're all that happy."

"I'm not," I tell her. "I'm lonely."

"Why is that? You have your brothers."

"I'm still lonely," I repeat. "Our father and mother have crossed the Dark River, and so has Christian, and I don't know what's become of them."

"They're with the King in his glorious City."

"Ah," I say, not wanting to sound rude, "but plenty of people say the stories about the King and the Celestial City aren't true."

"They really are true," Wisdom assures me. "That's why the King's Son has sent me to tell you to start your journey at once."

I shake my head. "My brothers . . ."

"You are to bring them with you," Wisdom says quickly. "The King's Son says he will take care of you all."

"So many of us?" I can't really believe what I'm hearing. I wonder if the King knows what my brothers are like. I wonder if he knows what *I'm* like.

Wisdom smiles. "The King's City is large, and there's room in it for every pilgrim who comes to the Gates. Imagine how pleased your parents will be when they hear that those Golden Gates are being opened for *you*!"

I can feel tears coming into my eyes, but I quickly wipe them away. "I'll think about it," I say, looking away from Wisdom and losing interest.

"Perhaps this will help you." Wisdom draws out a folded sheet paper.

I'm interested now. "What is it?" I ask.

"It's a letter from the King. Keep it safe and read it often."

"What does it say?" I have to know, but my eyes are running too much to see it clearly.

"It's a promise from the King. To you."

"For me?" I turn away to hide my tears. Not only is Wisdom being kind, but the King has even sent me a letter.

"I'll read it," I promise. Then I think for a moment. "But I'm still lonely."

Part 2 - Christiana's Story

CHAPTER 2
My Brothers

I'm still finding it hard to believe that the letter is for me. As I read it, my heart fills with joy mixed with unhappiness – joy that the King should send me such a loving message, and unhappiness that I've never even bothered with him before.

I look up again at Wisdom, who is standing near me. "I'll go," I say, after a moment of thought, "and I'll try to persuade my brothers to go with me."

Wisdom smiles. "I'm glad," she says. "Don't wait any longer, Christiana. The way is easier for young people, and the King's Son will help you in your difficulties."

"Difficulties?" That surprises me. I'm not sure I want too many difficulties. "Can you go with us? I won't be frightened if you show us the way."

Wisdom smiles. "No, Christiana, I have other work to do. But there's no need to be frightened. The King's Son will watch over you. Did you see a light in the distance, when you were on the hill?"

I nod my head.

"That light marks the path to the Wicket Gate. After you've gone through the Gate, you'll meet many of the King's servants who are there to help you."

Wisdom goes, and I keep reading that letter. In the evening I show it to Matthew and Samuel, the oldest two of my four brothers. "What do you think?" I ask.

"I think you ought to go," Samuel says. Although he's nearly twelve, I always think of him as being the most sensible brother I have.

"I'd like to go, but what will happen to you boys if I leave you alone?" I ask.

"We'll go with you," Matthew, the oldest of the four, says immediately. "At any rate *I* will."

"Will you really?" I give him a hug. Matthew is only a year younger than me, but he's not as thoughtful as Samuel.

"I've often thought about going," Matthew tells me. "You know, since our father and mother crossed the Dark River. When Christian went away, I was half inclined to follow him. It will be good for us all to go together."

I smile as I look into the fire. "Our parents will certainly be pleased to see us. But I don't know what to do about Joseph and James." James is eight, and probably too young for such an adventure.

The door flies open, and my two youngest brothers rush in. "What are you three talking about?" James asks.

"Christiana has a letter," Samuel tells him, as he puts it on the table where both brothers can read it.

Part 2 - Christiana's Story

"Look, it's from the King," Joseph says excitedly. "Why has he written to you, Christiana?"

"Who brought it?" James asks. "Did it *really* come from the King?"

"One of the visitors to the city brought it," I explain. "Her name is Wisdom. I'm sure you've seen her in the streets."

"I know her," Joseph says. "She spoke to me the other day, and I liked her. So are you going?" He comes round to the fire and leans against my chair, looking into my face.

"If I do, will you come with me, Joseph?" I ask.

"I don't mind. Will we have to fight anybody? Are there any wild beasts?"

"I don't know, but Wisdom says the King's Son will watch over us. We have to pass through a Wicket Gate with the light over it. Do you remember hearing how Pliable went with Christian, and both of them fell into the Slough of Despond."

Joseph pulls a face. "That terrible place?"

"What is it?" James asks.

"It's a great bog like quicksand that sucks people down," Joseph says, and he makes a loud sucking noise in an attempt to frighten his younger brother.

"Then *we'll* be careful," Samuel says. Yes, he's by far the most sensible of all my brothers, and I think he's also the bravest.

"I'd like to be a pilgrim, Christiana," Joseph tells me, jumping up and down, "but what about James? You can't leave *him* behind."

"No," I tell him, "of course we can't." I have to smile, for at nine Joseph is only a year older than James. If Joseph can make it, surely James can too.

"Does that mean we're all going?" Joseph asks. "Please say we are, Christiana. Please."

I nod happily. "If that's what you want."

"When can we start? Tomorrow?" Joseph is still jumping up and down.

I want to jump up and down too, but as their sister I have to behave a little more sensibly. "The next day, I think. We can prepare everything at night and leave early, as soon as the gates of our city are opened."

Part 2 - Christiana's Story

CHAPTER 3
Leaving Home

This will be my last afternoon in the City of Destruction, and one of my best friends has come to see me. Her name is Mercy. She's thirteen, the same age as Matthew. Unfortunately, Mercy's mother has come as well. We call her mother Mrs. Bats-Eyes, but of course not to her face. James thought of the name last year, and I told him it's extremely rude to make up names for people. But we all use it now. I don't think Mercy knows it's what we call her mother. At least, I hope she doesn't. Mercy has a much older sister called Bountiful. Bountiful is married, but not happily, I think, and I'm not even sure where she's living.

Mrs. Bats-Eyes has a habit of saying, "I can't see this, I can't see that," whenever anyone has an idea she doesn't agree with. She has a friend we call Mrs. Know-Nothing, and I'm glad to say she hasn't come this afternoon.

"Oh, you *do* look busy, Christiana," Mrs. Bats-Eyes says. "We're here to invite you to go with us to the country tomorrow."

"I don't think I can," I say, not wanting to reveal too much about my plans. "I have so many things to do at the moment."

"I can't see that matters. Not if you want to be with Mercy," Mrs. Bats-Eyes says. "No, I can't see it at all."

I'm glad my brothers are out. They would all be looking at each other and giggling by now.

"You're packing everything away," Mercy says. "Are you getting ready for a journey, Christiana?"

I've not planned to say anything about the King's letter, but now I feel it would be better to say what I'm going to do.

"I've received a message from the King," I say, "and I'm going to the Celestial City."

"Oh," Mrs. Bats-Eyes cries, "I can't see that's a sensible thing to do at all."

"I'd like you to come with me, Mercy," I say, avoiding her mother's eyes.

"And leave this beautiful city and all her friends?" Mrs. Bats-Eyes gives a loud snort. "I can't see why Mercy would want to do that, Christiana. And what will your brothers do? It's wrong of you to think of leaving them."

"I'm not leaving them. They're coming with me."

Mrs. Bats-Eyes laughs. "You must be mad, girl. How can boys like Joseph and James be pilgrims? We all know about your friend Christian and his troubles. He was nearly lost in the Slough of Despond. How do you think that place got its name?"

"Because it's like a marsh," I say, worried now that Mercy's mother might talk me out of going.

Part 2 - Christiana's Story

"The Slough of . . . *Despond.*" Mrs. Bats-Eyes emphasizes the last word. "It's called that because people want to give up when they get there. And by the look of you, Christiana, you're ready to give up now – before you've even started! No, I really can't see it's a good idea."

I shake my head, deliberately. A moment ago I had indeed thought about giving up, but not any longer. "I've made my mind up to go," I say firmly. I want to tell Mrs. Bats-Eyes that *she* made it up for me by being so annoying, but I think better of it.

Mrs. Bats-Eyes hasn't finished. "Remember when Mistrust and Timorous came back? They told us that Christian had met *lions* on Hill Difficulty."

"I'm not afraid of lions," I say, but of course I am.

"Yes," Mrs. Bats-Eyes continues, "and you can't have forgotten the news from Vanity Fair about the death of young Faithful. You're stupid to run into such danger, Christiana – especially with four brothers who need you to take care of them."

"Matthew's thirteen, and big enough now to take care of *me*," I tell her. "Anyway, the King's Son will watch over us. Look, here's the King's letter. You can read it if you like."

But Mrs. Bats-Eyes won't even look at it, so I pass it to Mercy.

Mrs. Bats-Eyes stands up. "It's no use wasting our time here," she tells Mercy. "You can go if you want, Christiana, but you'll soon be back!"

Mercy is usually much more ready to speak up for me, but today she seems strangely quiet. I'm not sorry when the door closes and I'm alone again. But only for a moment, for Joseph and James burst in and ask me if anything's the matter.

I tell them how Mercy's mother has been doing her best to talk us out of going to the Celestial City, and they're not to be bothered about my tears.

"Mrs. Bats-Eyes is silly," Joseph says. "She can never see the sense in anything."

"I'm not taking any notice of her," I say. "But I'm glad Wisdom came here and spoke to me. If she hadn't, I don't think I'd be bothering to pack."

Samuel comes back for tea much sooner than usual to ask if he can help, eager for us to start our pilgrimage. Matthew, of course, is the last to return.

"I've washed and mended your clothes," I tell them, "but they're getting very shabby. You'll have to look after them carefully."

"Perhaps the King will send us some new ones," Samuel suggests.

"Perhaps he will," I say, but I don't think it's likely.

* * *

Very early in the morning we creep away from our cottage, and out through the gates of the city. The gatekeeper doesn't stop us. He probably thinks we're going to spend a long day in the meadows. Samuel and Matthew are carrying our belongings, and I have the food.

Part 2 - Christiana's Story

Joseph and James run on in front because they're anxious to get to the Wicket Gate.

"Maybe we'll meet a lion," Joseph calls back. "If we do, *I* won't be frightened."

"Nor will I," James adds, sounding fearless. "Pilgrims are *always* brave, and we must fight for Christiana."

I think it's more likely I'll be fighting for them – with the help of Matthew and Samuel, of course. I hear a shout, and turn to see Mercy running across the meadow.

"Stop," she cries. "*Please* let me speak to you, Christiana."

Mercy sounds out of breath, but she catches hold of my hand. "Can I walk a little way with you?" she asks.

"If you want to, you can travel with us all the way to the Celestial City," I tell her.

Mercy shakes her head. "I'd like to, but I don't think the King will let me into his City. He hasn't sent me a message."

That puzzles me, and all I can do is frown.

"You remember, Christiana, you showed me a letter from the King, and my mother laughed at you." Mercy looks unhappy.

"You don't need a letter," Samuel tells her. "Evangelist says the King wants *everyone* to become pilgrims."

But Mercy shakes her head. "I don't think the King will let me into his City – if he hasn't invited me."

"I'll tell you what we'll do," I say, having a sudden idea. "Come with us as far as the Wicket Gate, and we'll ask if it's all right for you to pass through."

Mercy agrees to this, and my brothers seem glad to have her with us – especially Matthew. We all go on together happily until we reach the edge of the Slough of Despond, a vast area of soggy marshland.

This is the place where I heard Pliable and Christian were nearly sucked under and drowned, which makes me more than a little worried – not that I'm going to tell the others. I say, "I don't know how we can get across. It seems so dangerous."

"I think we should try," Mercy says. "Let's not give up so easily."

The soft mud oozes out between the tufts of grass as we move our feet, but as we look around we catch sight of some stepping-stones. Samuel, the bravest, goes first, slowly checking that each stone is firm. Joseph and James follow him, skipping lightly from stone to stone.

We find ourselves on the far side on firm ground, and I don't think there are any other unsafe places between us and the Wicket Gate – as long as we make straight for the light.

"I want everyone to keep going, so let's walk quickly," I tell them. "Perhaps we can rest once we've gone through the Wicket Gate."

Part 2 - Christiana's Story

CHAPTER 4
The Wicket Gate

About the middle of the day, the six of us reach a strong door set into a high wall. Over the door I see the words: *Knock, and the door will be opened to you.* The bright light we saw in the distance shines out from these words that the King's Son has put there.

"You're the eldest," Matthew says to me, looking a little scared, "and the King's letter was for you, Christiana, so you'd better be the one to knock. Say who we are and why we've come."

I can understand why Matthew doesn't want to do the knocking himself, even though he seems to know exactly what to say. The Gate is huge and rather daunting. I lift a small hammer and knock, but no one answers. A dog starts to bark furiously somewhere behind us, and although I'm sure Joseph and James mean to be brave, they both turn pale, and whisper, "Can we go home?"

"There's nothing to be afraid of," Mercy says firmly, but I think she's as frightened as my two youngest brothers.

"Knock again," Samuel suggests, standing back with Matthew. "Louder this time."

So I lift the hammer and start knocking as hard as I can.

Suddenly a small door within the large one opens. This small door, I realize, is the Wicket Gate. Surely no one could open the large door, but this one is just big enough to let us through one at a time.

"My name is Goodwill," a pleasant man says. "Who are you?"

The dog hears his voice and leaves off barking.

"Please don't be annoyed with us," I say, trying to sound confident. "I kept knocking because I thought you couldn't hear us, and we were frightened of the dog."

Goodwill looks at us and smiles. "Where have you all come from, and what do you want me to do for you?"

"We've come from the City of Destruction where Christian used to live," I tell him, sounding a little braver now that I've seen Goodwill smile. "We want to be the King's pilgrims – if you'll let us pass through your Gate. These are my brothers."

Goodwill leads us through the Wicket Gate. "I always let young people come to me," he said.

I've seen words like these written in the Book Christian was so fond of reading, and know the King's Son himself spoke them. Just for a moment I wonder if Goodwill *is* the King's Son. Certainly, our welcome could not have come from anyone kinder. I smile with relief as I enter the Way of the King, with my brothers following one by one. The Wicket Gate closes behind us.

Part 2 - Christiana's Story

Suddenly a trumpet sounds out from high on the wall. Goodwill says he has told a man to play a tune of welcome to five new pilgrims. Five? There should be six of us. I can see my four brothers, so where's Mercy?

"Don't forget me," I hear someone call from outside the Wicket Gate, as the trumpeter finishes his piece.

I turn quickly to Goodwill. "We have a friend with us," I tell him. "She wants to go to the Celestial City, but the King hasn't sent her a letter, so she's afraid . . ."

I have no time to say anything more, for someone starts knocking frantically on the Wicket Gate.

"Is that her?" Goodwill asks.

It certainly sounds like her. "I think so," I say.

Goodwill throws the door open. "Are you all right?" he asks.

Mercy is lying on the ground. I think she's fainted with shock at the thought of being shut outside.

Goodwill stoops down and picks her up in his arms. "Don't be frightened," he says softly as Mercy opens her eyes. "Tell me why you've come."

Mercy looks pale. "I don't have a letter. I only came this far because my friend Christiana let me."

"Did Christiana invite you to go to the Celestial City with her?" Goodwill asks.

"Yes, and I'd like to go. Will the King be angry with me?"

Goodwill shakes his head. "My Gate is open to *everyone* who knocks on it. Didn't you see the promise written above the door?"

Mercy nods.

"And can you remember what it says?"

Mercy smiles up at him. "It says, 'Knock, and the door will be opened to you.' That's why I kept knocking."

"I put those words there specially for you," Goodwill tells her. "So of course you can come in."

He carries Mercy through the Wicket Gate to join us.

Part 2 - Christiana's Story

CHAPTER 5
Starting Out

Goodwill leads the way into a cool, quiet room where he says we can rest until he comes for us later.

As soon as we're alone, I turn to Mercy. "I'm glad we're all here."

"I think I ought to be more glad than any of you," Mercy says quietly.

"No," I tell her, "I think we're all just as glad. When I knocked on the door and nobody answered, I thought we'd had our long walk for nothing – especially when that dog started barking."

"The worst time for me was when you'd all gone in, and I was left behind," Mercy says, laughing a little now. Perhaps it's relief. "I didn't like to knock again, until I looked up and saw the words carved over the Gateway. Then I knocked as loudly as I could."

"Loudly?" I say. "I never heard such knocking in all my life. I thought you were going to break the door down!"

"Well," Mercy says, "I couldn't help it. The Wicket Gate was shut, and that fierce dog must have been somewhere near. *You* would have knocked loudly if you'd felt so frightened."

"I wonder why Goodwill keeps that noisy dog," I say. "If I'd known about it, I'm not sure I would have dared come. But we're all safe now, and I'm pleased."

"So am I," Mercy says. "I think I'll ask Goodwill why he allows such a savage animal anywhere near his Gate."

"Yes," Joseph says, "ask him, Mercy. James is afraid it will bite us when we leave here."

I have to smile. It's probably Joseph who's afraid of the dog, although he won't admit it. But maybe I'm a bit frightened myself. Perhaps we all are.

James pulls me to one side. "I like Goodwill," he says. "Do you think he's the King's Son?"

I don't laugh, which is probably what he's expecting me to do. I've been wondering the same thing ever since we came through the Wicket Gate.

Goodwill returns, and I'm about to ask him who he really is, but Mercy interrupts and wants to know why he keeps the dog.

"It's not mine," he says. "There's a dark palace not far from here. The dog belongs to the evil prince. It lives at the palace, but it can run along his master's land until it comes close to my cottage. Then, as soon as it hears pilgrims approaching, it begins to bark. The evil prince has taught it to do this. Once or twice it has even broken through the fence and bitten a pilgrim

Part 2 - Christiana's Story

before they could knock. But I always open the Wicket Gate as soon as I know someone really wants to come in."

I ask Goodwill about the Way of the King, and he's ready to answer all my questions. Afterwards he tells us to wash while he prepares a midday meal for us. At last we feel refreshed, and able to go on our journey.

As we stand in the road, Goodwill warns us that the boundary of the evil prince's garden runs along the Way of the King for the next few miles. He points to a high wall by the side of the road, and says it stops the savage dog seeing us. He assures us there's no way the dog can come near to hurt us now that we've passed through the Wicket Gate.

I see the branches of some trees hanging over the wall, making a pleasant shade from the sun. Some of the trees are full of ripe berries. As the branches are within easy reach, my brothers of course begin to pick the fruit.

"You shouldn't do that," I warn them. "It may be dangerous to eat. I've never seen fruit like it before, and that garden belongs to the evil prince."

My brothers already have their mouths full. "Delicious," Matthew says.

At least Joseph and James are wise enough to listen. They quickly spit their berries out and throw the rest away. I think Samuel has already eaten some, but he stops immediately.

"I'm as big as you," Matthew tells me scornfully. "And I know just as much as you do. This fruit is good." So he goes on eating.

CHAPTER 6
Danger

We've not gone far from the Wicket Gate when we see two older boys coming toward us. They are taller than Matthew, and are probably sixteen or seventeen years old. As soon as I see them, I feel uneasy. "I don't like the look of them," I say to Mercy. "Come on, let's keep walking and take no notice."

Matthew and Samuel are lagging a little way behind, complaining that they don't feel well. I wish they'd listened to me when I told them not to eat the berries. Matthew, though, is the one who's really suffering. The two boys are laughing and talking together. They stand in the middle of the path to stop us. Joseph and James whisper to me that they feel frightened, and I have no idea what to do.

I recall a strange dream I had a few days ago, in which two boys just like these tried to stop me making my journey. I woke up feeling frightened, and I'm feeling frightened now. And this isn't a dream.

The smaller of the two boys stands threateningly, with his hands on his hips. "Where are you going?" he demands.

Part 2 - Christiana's Story

"We're pilgrims," I tell him. "And we don't have any money, if that's what you want."

The taller boy grabs hold of my arm, and his companion catches hold of Mercy. "We don't want your money," he says in an unpleasant voice. "And we're not going to hurt you. You are two extremely pretty girls, and we want you to stay and be friends with us."

"We can't," I say loudly. "We're going to the King, and we've no time to spare."

"Oh, that's all nonsense," the taller boy replies. "Anyway, we're going to *make* you stay."

I know that if Matthew and Samuel hadn't been eating the fruit from the evil prince's garden they would at least *try* to defend us. But now I can see that not only are they in pain, they're as scared as Joseph and James.

I realize we aren't able to get away from these two, and I call out for help. I remember how loudly Mercy called when she was outside the Wicket Gate, and I tell her to shout with me.

We're not far from the Gate, and Goodwill hears us and sends a man to see what's happening. The man comes quickly, and as he gets near, he shouts to the boys, "What are you doing? How dare you obstruct the King's pilgrims?"

When the boys hear his voice they let us go free, and hurry to the wall. They climb it as fast as they can and drop into the evil prince's garden, which is where they probably came from. I feel so relieved to see them go that I keep thanking the man for coming to help us.

"You needn't thank me," he says, "but it's not a good idea for you to travel alone. I'm surprised you didn't ask Goodwill to send a guide with you. Your brothers aren't old enough to be of much use."

This makes Matthew and Samuel hang their heads in shame. Samuel seems to be recovering slightly, and I'm hoping he didn't eat too many berries. But I'm worried about Matthew.

"I thought I was going to be so brave," Matthew says, "but I'm really a coward."

"It's not your fault," I tell him. "We never thought about the danger. I wonder why Goodwill didn't send someone with us, if he knows it's not safe for us to be alone."

"The King doesn't allow Goodwill to send guides – unless the pilgrims ask for them," the man explains.

I already have a feeling I've made a mistake in starting out on this journey. "Perhaps we'd better all turn back," I say, "and tell Goodwill we're sorry."

"No, you mustn't turn back," the man says quickly. "It's not far to the house of a man called Interpreter. You can ask for a guide when you get there."

"This is dreadful," Mercy says when the man leaves us. "I thought once we'd started, we'd never have any trouble again."

I feel so wretched, standing in the road. "Oh, Mercy, we don't only have to take care of *ourselves*, I'm responsible for my brothers as well. I feel such a failure."

Part 2 - Christiana's Story

CHAPTER 7
The House of Interpreter

From now on we are going on our way much more carefully. Samuel is well again, Matthew says he's feeling better, and Joseph and James are keeping much closer to me than they did in the morning. Mercy says her feet are aching.

We see a large house in the distance, close to the road. "That must be the house of Interpreter," I tell the others brightly, hoping to make them feel better. "I'll ask if we can sleep there tonight."

"And we must ask for a guide," Mercy reminds me.

The windows are wide open, and as we come up the pathway to the house, we hear people talking. I fancy I catch the sound of my own name, so we stand to listen. I can hardly believe my ears. It seems that the people inside the house know we're coming, and are looking forward to seeing us.

They obviously don't know we're here already, so I knock on the door and a young woman comes to open it.

"Who do you wish to see?" she asks pleasantly.

My brothers and Mercy stand back. I seem to be the one who has to do all the talking when we meet people. "We were told this house belongs to one of the King's servants," I say. "Do you think we could stay until the morning? My brothers are tired, and they're afraid to go on traveling in the dark." Well, I might as well put the blame on them. They've not been particularly brave so far.

The young woman nods understandingly. Perhaps she has younger brothers as well. "You must tell me your names, and I will ask my master whether there is room for you in the house."

"My name is Christiana. I think a friend of mine called Christian stayed here when he was a pilgrim. These are my four brothers, and this is our friend, Mercy."

The young woman goes quickly to a large room where we can see a man sitting at a table with some very young pilgrims who are probably his children. "Can you guess who is at the door?" I hear her say. "It's Christiana, with her brothers and a friend."

The man pushes his chair back and hurries to the door to welcome us. "Come in, come in. My name is Interpreter. Are you really Christiana?" he asks. "Christian told us about you when he came here, and we heard you were on your way."

"Yes, I'm Christiana," I say, feeling embarrassed, and we all stay on the doorstep. I wish now that I'd started the journey with Christian, because it seems that all the good things he told me about in his Book are true.

"How pleased Christian will be when he meets you in the Celestial City," Interpreter says. "But we mustn't let you stand at the door. Come in and rest."

Interpreter tells us there are older pilgrims staying in the house, as well as his own family. He takes us into the large hall where everyone is sitting at a long table. They all seem pleased to see us, and two of the women stand up and give Mercy and me a kiss. They give Joseph and James a quick kiss too. The two boys are too polite to push the women away, but Joseph wipes his face hard afterwards. Matthew and Samuel must have guessed what was about to happen, and have gone to look out of the window.

Chris Wright

CHAPTER 8
Raking Straw

We've been resting for a short time, and now Interpreter is taking us to see a painting of the Good Shepherd. James seems to understand how the sheep in the picture was lost on the mountains, and in great trouble until the Good Shepherd found it and took it in his arms. We all stare at the painting, and it slowly dawns on us that this is the King's Son – and he looks exactly like Goodwill!

Interpreter takes us into a poorly lit room where a miserable-looking man is working hard. The floor of the room is covered with straw, and small sticks and dust. The man is holding a rake and using it to pull the rubbish into a heap. He doesn't look up when Interpreter opens the door, and he only seems interested in the rubbish.

"Why is he doing this?" Matthew asks.

I have no idea, and turn to Interpreter hoping he has the answer.

"This man keeps asking the King for riches, and now he believes all this rubbish is extremely valuable," Interpreter tells

Part 2 - Christiana's Story

Matthew, although all of us are listening to the answer. "The King is sorry for him, and every day he sends a messenger offering him a golden crown instead of the straw."

As Interpreter speaks, he points up. We raise our heads and notice an angel holding a bright crown.

"But he doesn't see it," Mercy says, frowning.

"No," Interpreter says. "That's because he won't look up."

I have to swallow hard. "I was just like this man," I say. "I always wanted things, and didn't care about the King and his City. But I *do* care now."

Interpreter nods. "There is only one person in a thousand who does not seek wealth," he said.

James is wriggling around in frustration. "Will he *never* look up?" he asks.

Joseph adds, "How long will the angel wait for him?"

"I cannot tell you," Interpreter tells them. "The King is patient, but the man is so sure he'll find treasure in the rubbish, that I don't know if he will *ever* look up."

Interpreter takes us next into a magnificent room and asks what we can see in it. I wonder if this a trick question, because the room is completely empty – apart from a spider dangling from the ceiling. I don't know what to say.

"There's nothing here," Mercy says, echoing the words I'd like to use – if it didn't make me sound foolish.

"I can see a spider," Joseph says. "A great big one."

I tell him not to be so rude.

"Only one spider?" Interpreter asks. "I can see seven." And he's looking at each of us in turn.

What does he mean? There are six of us, which makes seven if he's including the spider. "Do we all look as ugly as the spider?" I ask, rather annoyed with Interpreter. But before he can answer, I understand what he's saying. "That spider has a nasty bite," I say, "and we sometimes speak unpleasant things with our mouths. Am I right?"

Interpreter smiles. "You're very quick," he says.

I'm ashamed of things I've said in the past, and bite my lip. Mercy is blushing, and my brothers have covered their faces. They obviously feel as I do.

"There is still something you have not understood about the spider," Interpreter says with a smile. "This is a fine room, perhaps the finest in the house." He looks at us to see if we can see the point he's making.

I'm about to ask why such a magnificent room has a spider in it, but I don't want to sound impolite.

When we've all shaken our heads, Interpreter says, "You may be thinking that the spider doesn't deserve to be here, but we allow it to spin its web in this room. So, even though you often do wrong, the King will give you a wonderful place in the Celestial City – because you belong to him."

I start to cry when I realize how kind the King is, and I think Mercy is crying too. I'm not sure about my brothers, for I don't like to look at them and embarrass them by letting them see my tears of shame.

Interpreter takes us to another room filled with hens. Some are pecking at corn, and some are drinking from a bowl. Each time they fill their mouths, the hens lift their heads and look at the ceiling.

"Why are these hens like good pilgrims?" Interpreter asks.

"Because they look up as though to say thank you every time they get food and other good things," Samuel says. "So we should keep saying thank you to the King."

I'm proud of him. "Samuel's right, isn't he?" I say to Interpreter.

Interpreter nods and takes into the garden where there are borders filled with flowers. Interpreter tells us that the King's servants are like these flowers. "Some are tall and stately, and no one can help seeing how beautiful they are. Others are small, and perhaps their blossoms aren't even brightly colored, but they have a sweet scent." Interpreter goes on to say the gardener loves *all* his flowers, and puts each one in its best place in the garden.

"In the same way," he adds, "the King loves all his servants, and gives them each a special place in his Kingdom. Some have difficult and important work to do, and others have only straightforward work, but not one of them is forgotten."

A robin flies down and settles on a low branch. It has a large caterpillar wriggling in its beak. I look away in disgust. "I wish robins only ate crumbs and things," I say, wrinkling up my nose. "That's such a lovely caterpillar he's caught. I don't think I like robins any more."

"Perhaps Interpreter has another warning for us," Mercy says quietly, nudging me.

Interpreter hears. "Well said, Mercy," he says, as he chases the robin away. He must have realized it upset me.

I can't see any point to this. "You'll have to tell me what it means," I say.

"That robin is like people who say they are followers of the King," Interpreter explains. "When they are in the company of true followers, they do and say nice things, but when they are with the King's enemies they can do horrible things. It's what they do naturally."

I get the point now.

Interpreter asks me questions about my old home in the City of Destruction, and even persuades Mercy to tell him about the time she came to the house with her mother and saw the letter the King sent me. Mercy explains how she suddenly made up her mind to be a pilgrim, even though her friends laughed at first.

"So even though it upset my mother and father," Mercy tells Interpreter, "I knew I had to start that day."

"And do you have any regrets?" Interpreter asks.

Mercy shakes her head. "Not any more."

Part 2 - Christiana's Story

CHAPTER 9
Greatheart

In the morning, the light of the rising sun wakes me. I call the others and we all wash and dress quickly, eager to continue our journey.

But when we go downstairs, Interpreter says, "Before you eat, I want you all to take a bath."

Not me, surely, I think to myself. Maybe the boys have missed a bit here and there, but I've washed ever so carefully since I came to this house. I almost feel insulted.

"The bath I have for you is one you will not find in any other place," Interpreter says. "The water will wash you cleaner than you are able to clean yourselves."

So we take it in turns to take a bath in marvelous, pure water. Although I thought I was clean enough before, I come out feeling more wonderful and happy than I ever knew was possible. Somehow, all the aches in my joints from the journey, as well as the dirt from the past, have been washed away. I feel clean inside and out.

Interpreter says we look "fair as the moon" when he sees us, and puts a mark on our foreheads with a special seal. "Now you will know you belong to the King's family," he says. "And others will know it too."

I had no idea this was going to happen when we got up this morning, and I'm so glad we stopped here at Interpreter's house. But Interpreter hasn't finished yet.

"The clothes you are wearing are no good for traveling," he tells us. "We must give you some new ones."

I feel myself going red. "I'm ever so sorry," I say. "I washed and mended them as well as I could, but they're badly worn and I couldn't make new ones in time."

"You did your best," Interpreter tells me, "but even if they *were* new and clean, they would not be suitable. The King has provided clothes for all his pilgrims, and the he will not welcome you in any others."

Mercy and the boys receive spotless clothes to wear. Interpreter also has a set for me.

"Did Christian get some of these clothes?" I ask, but even as I put the question, I know I've made a mistake in asking it. Of course, Christian must have had them. How else could he have got into the Celestial City?

"Christian was given his clothes at the Cross," Interpreter says.

I look at my brothers and at Mercy, and when I see how good their clothes are, I feel almost frightened. "If the journey is long and difficult," I say to them, "how can we possibly keep these clothes clean until we reach the Gates of the City?"

Part 2 - Christiana's Story

Joseph and James stand still, gazing solemnly down at themselves. "We can never play anymore," they say to each other in dismay.

Interpreter smiles and draws the boys nearer to him. "Do not be afraid," he says. "The King loves to see his pilgrims happy. Your clothes will not be harmed, unless you quarrel or act in a foolish way. Run about as much as you like, as long as you do not leave the Way of the King."

I look at Mercy. "The King is so good," I tell her.

Mercy shakes her head slowly in disbelief. "I know I'm a true pilgrim now," she says, with tears in her eyes. "All this time I've been afraid, because I entered the Wicket Gate without receiving a message from the King. But now look at me – I'm clothed in garments from his own treasury. Oh, the King is so good to me, I could cry for joy."

"You *are* crying for joy," I say, giving Mercy a hug.

"You are washed clean," Interpreter says, "and clothed with righteousness through the King's Son."

Interpreter gives each of us a piece of rolled up paper. ""These are your Rolls of Faith," he explains. "You must look after them carefully, because you will need to show them at the entrance to the Celestial City. You are in the King's family, and are his forever."

We prepare to leave, and Interpreter hands me a parcel. "This is for the next part of your journey," he says. "I've put a pomegranate and a piece of honeycomb in there for you all. And there is also something to drink."

He calls one of his young servants whose name is Greatheart, and says to him, "I want you to go with these pilgrims to the House Beautiful, and take care that none of the King's enemies hurt them on the Way."

Greatheart is a tall, pleasant-looking young man. He's wearing a suit of bright armor and carries a sword at his side. I feel sure he'll be able to protect us if we meet with any danger.

Interpreter and his family come to the door and watch us set off. Greatheart leads the way, while Joseph and James stay close behind him. I'm walking with Mercy and Samuel, and some way behind us is Matthew.

I turn to see why he's dropping back. "Is anything wrong?" I call.

Matthew shakes his head.

"Well, you're looking poorly." A sudden thought occurs to me. "Are you still feeling ill from eating those berries?"

"I don't think so," Matthew says.

"Don't think so, indeed," I say. "Well, I hope it isn't far to the House Beautiful."

"So do I," Matthew says, clutching his stomach and dropping even further back.

Part 2 - Christiana's Story

CHAPTER 10
The Cross

We have only been going for a short time, and already we've come to the Cross on a small hill. Greatheart says we can stop here for a rest. We sit down on the grass and Greatheart tells us how Christian's burden fell from his shoulders when he got here.

"Christian was forgiven by the King's Son when he entered the Wicket Gate," Greatheart explains, "but he still felt the burden of all the things he'd done wrong in the past. But when he came here to the Cross he understood that the King's Son had taken everything from him, so he need not feel guilty any longer."

I have all sorts of questions for Greatheart about the King's Son, and all he's done for us. Greatheart obviously loves the King's Son, and seems willing to talk about him.

"Didn't you recognize the King's Son when he let you through the Wicket Gate?" Greatheart asks.

I almost jump with surprise. "The only person we saw was Goodwill." I remember how James asked me if Goodwill was the King's Son. I'd even started to put the question to Goodwill, but Mercy asked him about the dog and it went out of my mind.

"If you saw Goodwill, then you saw the King's Son," Greatheart says with a broad smile. "They are indeed the same person. Who else do you think could let you into the Way of the King, but the King's Son?"

"But I didn't . . ." I start to say.

"You didn't thank him enough." Greatheart finishes the sentence for me. "Don't worry, Christiana, the King's Son knows all about you, and he loves you. It is he who has forgiven you for all the things you have ever done wrong, and it is he who has washed you clean, and it is he who will receive you into his Father's City."

"Why is there a Cross?" Joseph asks.

"A good question, and one that not everybody understands," Greatheart says. "The King was once angry with every person in the City of Destruction, and he wanted to punish them for doing wrong. But his Son has taken the terrible punishment instead, on this Cross. So now the King can offer forgiveness and cleansing to everyone who asks him for it."

To think we actually saw the King's Son when we entered the Way of the King, and didn't realize it. Well, I believe James did. I keep thinking back to the time at the Wicket Gate, wanting to see Goodwill again, so I can remember him more clearly.

"What are those pieces of paper?" I ask, noticing things nailed to the Cross.

Part 2 - Christiana's Story

"They are lists of all the things each one of you has ever done wrong," Greatheart says. "Why don't you go and read the one with your name on it?"

Why don't I? Why would I want to be reminded of all those things? I'd much rather the King forgot about them! But I can't resist having a look, so I go forward cautiously, as though afraid of being bitten, and get the piece of paper with my name on it.

"It's blank!" I say in surprise. "There's nothing written on it!"

"Maybe you weren't listening just now," Greatheart says with a smile. "Because his Son died on the Cross, the King offers forgiveness and cleansing to everyone who asks. His Son was punished instead of you, Christiana, so all the wrong things you have ever done are now forgiven and forgotten. They are washed away, so the paper is blank."

For the first time ever, I understand what it means to be forgiven by the King. I break down in tears and kneel in front of the Cross to say thank you. I don't look at my brothers or Mercy, but I can hear them doing the same, for every piece of paper is blank.

The time slips quickly away, and we feel almost sorry when we have to leave this quiet resting place.

Not far from the Cross we find some chains, hanging on a post by the side of the road. Greatheart says this is where Christian found three boys called Simple, Sloth and Presumption, sleeping on the grass with their feet bound in these chains. They didn't listen to him when he woke them and told them to keep going, and in the end he had to leave them here. Greatheart says they never tried to undo their chains, for they had no wish to continue their journey.

So all day long the three sat idly by the road, doing everything they could to upset the King's pilgrims by trying to persuade them to leave the right path. In the end, they caused so much trouble that the King lost patience with them and ordered them to be taken away.

Greatheart points to the chains. "People can see them here, and be warned not to try to delay other pilgrims," he explains.

I close my eyes for a moment and try to imagine Christian standing on this bit of the path, talking to those three boys. "I'm glad they didn't persuade Christian to leave the Way," I say aloud.

"And it's a good thing they aren't still here," Mercy says. "If we didn't have Greatheart with us, they might have talked us into giving up."

The road brings us to the foot of a hill where I find a spring of water bubbling up inside a deep pool. I'm feeling thirsty, so I bend down to catch some water in my hands.

Greatheart shakes his head. "Don't drink it," he says. "Not long ago this pool was clear as crystal. But some of the evil prince's servants found the spring, and they think it's fun to make it unfit for the King's pilgrims to drink. So every time they come past they kick dirt into it, to make it too muddy for anyone to drink."

I remember packing a cup in Matthew's bag, and Greatheart tells me to fill it with water from the pool and wait for the dirt to settle. After a few minutes the water looks clear and bright, so we take it in turns to drink carefully from the cup, and feel refreshed.

A path goes up the middle of the hill. It's marked *The Way of the King*. Greatheart says this is Hill Difficulty, and he shows us two paths made by the evil prince, both blocked off with posts and chains. One path is marked *Danger*, and it leads into a dark forest, and the other is marked *Destruction* and goes towards some treacherous mountains.

"Formality and Hypocrisy were lost down those two paths," Greatheart tells us, "but Christian climbed the King's path up the hill. Since then, the King has sent men to put these warnings across the wrong paths. Even so, some pilgrims can't see the danger and ignore the signs, because the paths look so easy."

CHAPTER 11
Hill Difficulty

As we go up the hill, Greatheart holds onto James, and the rest of us help each other as much as we can. The track is steep and rough, and the sun's rays beat down fiercely on our heads.

Presently Mercy groans loudly. "What a dreadful way up. I don't think I can walk another step. Let's sit down for a few minutes."

James hears Mercy, and he too asks to stop. He's been doing his best to climb the hill, but he keeps falling, and his hands and knees are bruised and sore.

"We can't rest here," Greatheart says.

This makes us all sigh loudly.

Greatheart smiles. "Don't worry, we're near a place the King has made for his pilgrims. Just keep hold of my hand, James. You've climbed bravely, and we're already past the worst. And, Joseph, you hold onto my other hand."

James looks happier when he hears Greatheart's words. "It's harder to go uphill than it is to go down," he says.

Part 2 - Christiana's Story

"But going downhill too fast can sometimes lead to difficulties," Samuel tells him, which I think is a pretty clever observation.

I'm learning quickly that taking the easy way can lead to big troubles. "I would much rather be going *up* a hill to the King's City, than *down* toward the evil prince's country," I say.

"Well said," Greatheart agrees, "and when you reach the King's City you'll be so happy that you'll forget all the trouble you've had on your journey."

Clasping his fingers tightly round those of his guide, James climbs briskly. In a few minutes a pleasant shelter comes in sight, and we hurry towards it.

"Oh," Mercy sighs, "it *is* good to rest when you're tired. Our King is kind to make such a cool shady place for his pilgrims."

"You see," Greatheart tells us, "the King's Son has traveled this path himself, so he knows how hard it is, and understands why pilgrims need a resting place." He calls Joseph and James and asks them how they like their pilgrimage.

"I didn't like it at all just now," Joseph says, sounding especially grown up, "but I must thank you for helping me."

"Would you like something to eat while you're resting?" I ask everyone. "When we were leaving his house, Interpreter gave us a pomegranate and a piece of honeycomb, and something to drink."

"I didn't like to ask what he was giving you," Mercy says, laughing. "I thought it might be something you wouldn't want to share."

"I think the King wants us to share everything," I say, as I unpack the food and divide it among all of us, asking Greatheart to take some. But the young soldier refuses, saying he'll be going back to Interpreter later, where there will be plenty of food for him.

"You're young pilgrims," he says, "so you must make the most of what has been provided for you."

Part 2 - Christiana's Story

CHAPTER 12
Lions!

We sit quietly in the King's shelter, eating our food and talking happily together, while Greatheart stands in the doorway. "We mustn't rest too long," he warns us. "We still have some distance to go before we reach the top of the hill, and the sun will soon be setting."

Joseph and James spring up at once, and start off ahead of everyone. All their bravery seems to have come back, and I hear them whispering to each other that they won't mind if they *do* meet a lion.

"Greatheart says the King is good, and we know he took care of Christian," I hear Joseph say.

James agrees. "And if we love him, I don't think there's any need to feel frightened."

When I see my two young brothers set off so quickly, I try to keep up with them. We didn't finish the bottle of refreshing drink just now, and I feel thirsty. I suddenly realize I must have left it in the King's shelter where we were eating.

I call to Samuel, and ask him to run back to look for it. While we're waiting, Greatheart says, "That's the place where

Christian lost his Roll of Faith. It seems to be a forgetting place for some pilgrims."

He tells us about other pilgrims who had to turn back to look for something they left there. I ask Greatheart why that should be.

"It's because they're careless," Greatheart tells me. "They get tired climbing the hill, and their rest makes them feel comfortable and happy. Often they sit there too long, and forget about the King – or even fall asleep. Then they jump up in such a hurry that they're almost sure to drop something without noticing."

Samuel returns with the bottle in his hand, and before going any further we all make sure we have our Rolls of Faith.

We're climbing steadily up the hill, when Greatheart stops. "Lions," he says say, signaling to us to stay back.

"Where?" we all ask together in fright.

Greatheart laughs. "I didn't mean to alarm you," he says, "but this is where Christian met Mistrust and Timorous. They frightened him by saying they'd seen two lions on the hill."

"Are the lions here now?" Joseph asks.

Greatheart stands with his sword in his hands. "Yes, but there's no need to be scared of them."

Joseph looks at his three brothers. "I don't want to meet a lion," he says shakily. "It might be *very* fierce. We'd better keep behind Greatheart."

"You loved going in front when there was no danger, and now you love to go last," Greatheart says to them, but I know he's only joking.

Part 2 - Christiana's Story

The sun has already set, and the shadows are deepening every moment. As we go forward slowly, two lions jump out of the bushes and roar loudly. Joseph and James scream equally loudly and begin to shake with fear. They hide behind

Greatheart who has drawn his sword, holding it in his hand ready to strike the lions if they spring forward.

"The beasts are chained," Greatheart says after a moment.

I can see the chains now, glistening in the darkness. "The path between them looks so narrow," I say, trying to sound brave so as not to worry my brothers.

"Keep in a single line in the center of the path," Greatheart tells us. "I can't pretend otherwise, but these savage creatures sometimes try to seize pilgrims."

Mercy gasps and puts her hand to her mouth. "Look, there's a terrible giant standing behind the lions."

Greatheart stops. "I know who he is," he tells us. "His name is Grim. He's made a home for himself here, and he's taught the lions to frighten any pilgrims who are passing."

Giant Grim sees us and steps into the narrow path, holding the manes of the two lions. Greatheart strides boldly forward, but we all stand back, waiting to see what is going to happen.

"What business have you to walk on this path?" the giant roars.

Greatheart raises his sword, "I am taking these young pilgrims to the Celestial City."

"This isn't the way to the City," Grim shouts "If you try to get past, and I will make my lions tear you in pieces."

I look in front and can see grass growing up thorough the stone path. The giant must have frightened the King's pilgrims so much that hardly anyone come this way now. I wonder if they've forgotten that the King's Son will take care of them. I remember what Wisdom told me before I left home, and call out, "We're not afraid. Our King's Son is with us, and he'll bring us safely past your lions."

When Giant Grim hears my voice he laughs, and says we're not going another step further towards the Celestial City.

Greatheart keeps on his way, and we creep after him. His armor glints in the shadows. In a moment his sword flashes through the air, and the giant moves back a few paces.

"Do you think you can *kill* me on my own ground?" Grim shouts at us.

"This path belongs to the King," Greatheart tells him. "Stand and defend yourself. If you won't let these young pilgrims pass, I will fight you for them."

CHAPTER 13
Watchful

Greatheart raises his sword as Giant Grim stoops down to unfasten the lions' chains. But before the giant can release them, Greatheart's sharp weapon crashes through the giant's helmet and he falls on his knees. He tries to get up, but with another blow from his sword Greatheart cuts off one of the giant's arms. Then Giant Grim roars so hideously that his voice scares us all, and we are glad to see him lie sprawling on the ground.

With a powerful blow from his sword, Greatheart cuts off the giant's head. James says, "Wow!" and Greatheart turns round to look for us. Mercy has hidden her face, but I was watching every moment of the battle, though when the giant roared with pain I couldn't help feeling sick. Greatheart holds out his hand to me.

"Come," he says confidently, "there's no danger now. We're nearly at the House Beautiful. Keep close to me and the lions won't hurt you. Their master is dead, and they're too frightened to spring at anyone."

Part 2 - Christiana's Story

We see the lions cowering on the ground as we follow Greatheart to the lodge, inside the gates of the large house. A man holding a lantern looks out of a window and asks who we are.

"Greetings, Watchful. It is I, Greatheart," our guide calls.

"I recognize you," Watchful says. "Wait there, I will come down and open the gate."

A few moments later Watchful unlocks the heavy gates. "How now, Greatheart, what is your business here so late tonight?" he asks.

"I have brought some pilgrims here to stay," Greatheart says, pointing to us. "I know I'm late, but the giant who used to look after the lions caused us some trouble."

"Used to look after the lions?" Watchful asks. "Do you mean to say Giant Grim is dead?"

"Greatheart cut his arm off," Joseph said.

"And he smashed the giant's head open with his sword," James adds. "Then he cut it right off. It was ever so exciting."

It's excitement I could have done without, but I'm glad the danger is over – not just for us, but for other pilgrims who will be coming this way later.

"Are you going to stay the night as well, Greatheart?" Watchful asks.

James goes close to Greatheart and grips his hand, "Please, please stay with us. I'll never forget how brave you've been, and how much you've helped us."

"I will go with you gladly," Greatheart tells him, "but I must first seek permission from Interpreter, my master. I have to go back tonight, but I'll tell him what you say, and perhaps he will let me come to you again. You should have begged him to let me go on with you, and I'm sure he would have granted your request. However, at present, I must withdraw. So, good Christiana, Mercy and my brave boys, farewell."

Greatheart is soon out of sight, for it's now completely dark.

Watchful turns to me and asks who I am, and where I've been living. I tell him, and he seems pleased to hear I was Christian's friend. He says everyone in the house liked Christian when he stayed here, and they've always remembered how he told them about me.

Watchful takes us across to the house and rings the front doorbell. The young woman who answers it goes quickly back inside with Watchful's message. I hear a commotion in the house, and my name is being called out in great excitement.

A girl who says her name is Prudence hurries out with two other girls to welcome us. Prudence explains that they have often talked about Christian, and are excited to know that I'm here now. She tells us that their oldest sister, Discretion, has gone away to work for the King in another place. The other two sisters introduce themselves as Piety and Charity. They kiss us in welcome, and this time even the boys seem to welcome their attention.

Part 2 - Christiana's Story

CHAPTER 14
Mercy's Dream

We feel exhausted and want to go straight to bed, but Prudence insists we have something to eat first. I think she's probably right, for food will help rebuild our strength.

"Supper is ready," Prudence calls, when we've all had a wash. She leads us through the large hall. "I don't think we ought to tire you out tonight with too much talking. I want you to sleep well, and tomorrow you can tell us about your journey."

There is so much food that it looks as though Prudence has been expecting us. "Did you hear we were coming?" I ask.

Prudence smiles. "Yes," she says, "news travels fast when pilgrims are on the Way. And you are of course welcome to our hospitality."

Prudence speaks so gently that I take courage, and say, "I don't know if I ought to ask for anything, but if you'd let me sleep with Mercy in the room where my friend Christian slept, we'd be so happy."

Prudence says no one is using the room, and she'll be pleased to let us have it. She adds that she'll give the adjoining room to my four brothers.

I lie awake for a long time, talking quietly with Mercy in the bed opposite about all that's happened since we left the City of Destruction. I tell her I can remember the day I first heard that Christian started his journey. "I didn't think I'd ever be a pilgrim myself," I add.

Mercy laughs. "And you never thought you'd stay in this grand house, and sleep in the room where Christian slept."

This makes me sigh. "In a way he was like one of my own brothers. I was so upset when he went away, but I'm happy now I know he's with the King. Isn't it wonderful? Some day I'll meet Christian in the Celestial City."

"Listen," Mercy says suddenly, "I can hear music. I'm sure I can. And singing too. Did you ever hear anything so beautiful?"

We lie still, while below in the hall the King's servants sing his praises before they go to rest. The music stops and we whisper good night to each other and I close my eyes, feeling happier than I've ever felt before.

* * *

I'm awake now, and daylight is streaming through the window. I tell Mercy she was laughing in her sleep. "Did you have a dream?" I ask.

Mercy's eyes shine, "I had a lovely dream. Did I really laugh?"

Part 2 - Christiana's Story

Did she! She woke me up several times in the night with her laughter. "What did you dream about?" I ask, laughing myself now.

Mercy's eyes are shining with delight. "It was strange, Christiana. I dreamt I was all alone, crying because I kept thinking what a bad person I was inside, and I knew I wasn't fit to be calling myself a pilgrim. Some of my friends came and demanded to know why I was crying. When I told them that my life wasn't pleasing to the King, they made fun and pushed me about, which made me cry even more."

I nod encouragingly at Mercy, willing her to go on. The dream must have had a big effect on her, although it doesn't sound like anything to laugh about. Not so far, anyway.

Mercy nods – more to herself than to me, I think. "At last I looked up and saw an angel coming down, who said, 'What's the matter, Mercy?'"

I almost feel jealous of Mercy for getting a dream about an angel. "What did you tell the angel?" I ask.

Mercy smiles. "I told him I felt miserable. Then he said, 'Peace be to you,' and wiped my eyes with his handkerchief, and dressed me in silver and gold. He put a chain round my neck, and earrings in my ears, and a beautiful crown on my head Then he took me by the hand, and said, 'Mercy, come after me.' So he went up, and I followed until we came to some Golden Gates."

"What happened?" I ask, for I've never had a dream anything like this.

Mercy is smiling now, as though she's remembering something good. "The angel knocked, and when the Gates were opened we went in. I followed the angel up to the King's throne, where the King said to me, 'Welcome, my daughter.' The place looked bright and twinkling, like the stars, or rather like the sun. And then I woke up. Are you sure I laughed?"

"Yes, and I don't wonder, when you had such a good dream," I tell her.

"Well," she says, "I hope it won't be long before I really see the King on his throne."

I'm so glad to hear Mercy's dream, but I think it must be time for us to get up, and I'm going to try to wake the boys.

Part 2 - Christiana's Story

CHAPTER 15
The Sisters

"If they invite us to stay here for a few nights, let's accept," Mercy says as we get dressed. "I'd like to get to know Prudence, Piety and Charity better."

"We'll have to see what they want us to do," I tell her, wishing deep down that we can indeed stay a little longer.

After breakfast, Prudence asks if we slept well. Mercy's eyes light up and she answers quickly, as though she's been planning what to say. "We did. This is the best place I've ever stayed in."

Prudence looks pleased. "You can stay for a few weeks, if you think you'll be happy here."

"Oh, yes," I say excitedly. "We'd enjoy it enormously."

We agree to spend a whole month at the House Beautiful, and during this time many good things happen. Sometimes Prudence calls my brothers together to find out what they know. I've been trying to teach them more about the King and his Son, and I'm pleased to hear them answer so well. All except Matthew.

For some reason I can't understand, Matthew refuses to listen to Prudence or answer her questions. Now I come to think of it, Matthew has been moody ever since we came through the Wicket Gate. I hope he's not going to be ill.

"You must always try to remember what your sister teaches you," Prudence says. "Then you'll be able learn more about the King and his Son. You're all so fond of reading, and that's a good thing, but you can be sure you'll never find anything better than the King's Book that Christian loved so dearly. There are stories in it for pilgrims of all ages, and wise teaching from the King's Son himself. The more you read it, the more you will grow to love it, for it will teach you how to serve the King faithfully."

Mercy has always been good with the needle and thread, and it isn't long before she organizes the three sisters into a sewing circle, making and mending clothes that can be given to those in need. When I see them hard at work I offer to join in, and soon we have quite a pile of clothing ready for ironing. When we run out of material, somehow Mercy seems to find something to patch up with her needle and thread.

One afternoon a boy named Brisk calls at the house. He seems bright and good-natured, but although he sometimes mentions the King and his Son, I can't help thinking he's only doing it to keep in with the three sisters. I also think he's rather fond of Mercy.

When he goes home I ask Prudence and her sisters about him, and they tell me they're hoping he'll become a true servant of the King. It seems he often calls at the house, but Prudence

Part 2 - Christiana's Story

has never been able to persuade him to become a pilgrim. He says he's too busy to find time to begin his journey. I remember Christian saying the same thing about his own father, and wonder if he's started his journey to the King.

Brisk comes in one morning and sits close to Mercy. He tells her he thinks she's the most beautiful girl he's ever seen, and invites her to go with him to meet his brothers and sisters. Mercy is busy sewing, and says she has a great deal of work to do.

Brisk comes to the house nearly every day to talk to Mercy, and tell her how pretty she is.

"He's a pleasant boy," Mercy tells me, "but he won't be a good friend for me if he doesn't love the King."

So whenever Brisk comes, she makes sure she has plenty of sewing to do, and doesn't take much notice of him.

CHAPTER 16
Matthew's Illness

Brisk looks upset when he realizes Mercy doesn't want to bother with him, and one day he says to her, "You're *always* too busy sewing to talk to me."

Mercy looks up, smiling. "Yes," she says, "there's always plenty to do."

"How much do you get paid?" Brisk asks.

Mercy smiles. "I don't do it for money."

"What *do* you do it for, then?"

"I'm making some clothes for Charity. She gives them to people in need."

Brisk seems surprised, and Mercy can't help looking across at me and smiling. Brisk sees us smiling and tells Mercy, yet again, that she's very pretty, but this time he's not coming back, as she must have something wrong with her head if she has such foolish ideas about helping the poor.

Mercy tells me she's not sorry to see him go. "I don't want any special friends who don't serve the King," she tells me. "Do you remember my sister Bountiful?"

Part 2 - Christiana's Story

I do. It's a sad story and one that I never like to ask Mercy about. Bountiful got married, and it seemed such a happy marriage at first.

"She married someone like Brisk," Mercy says. "She was a pilgrim, and wanted to work for the King. But her husband wanted her to do nothing except look after him. I think he was jealous of the help she gave other people. She told him she was helping others before she married, and she was going to carry on doing it."

I remember hearing about it at the time, but it was quite a few years ago and I probably never knew the full details. "What happened," I ask, for Mercy seems willing to talk about it now.

"Her husband threw her out of the house and told her to go and live with the poor, if she loved them so much."

This shocks me. "I thought he was a pilgrim too," I say.

"He said he was," Mercy says. "That's why my sister married him. But I think he was only pretending, so he could marry her."

"Then you did well to turn Brisk away when you did," I say, looking at Mercy. She seems to have grown up a lot since we started out, and I can see why any young man would want her as a friend. "There are probably a lot of men like that around."

Mercy laughs. "You'd better warn your brothers," she says. "They'll probably meet a lot of girls who pretend to be pilgrims too."

* * *

I'm worried about Matthew. Every morning now when he gets up he says his head aches, and he often feels so sick and faint he finds it hard to stand.

Today he can hardly lift his head from his pillow when I go to wake him. I run back to my room to finish dressing, so I can ask Prudence what to do. Prudence sends at once for a doctor, an old man called Dr. Skill. He arrives quickly, and I take him upstairs to see my brother.

Matthew is lying in bed, and Joseph is sitting by him, for the two are fond of each other.

"What has he been eating?" Dr. Skill asks.

"Nothing but wholesome food," I tell him.

The doctor shakes his head. "Your brother has been eating some sort of poison, and if the medicine I give him won't take effect, he will die,"

I feel so worried that I'm unable to speak, but Samuel cries out, "It must be the berries. They were hanging over the wall after we went through the Wicket Gate, and Matthew ate some. Remember, Christiana, you made us throw them away?"

I remember now. "I told Matthew not to eat them," I say, "but he wouldn't listen to me, and kept putting them into his mouth."

"Ah," Dr. Skill says, "I knew he had eaten something poisonous. That fruit is worse than any other, for it grows in the evil prince's own garden. Your brother won't be the first pilgrim to die from eating it."

Part 2 - Christiana's Story

I feel tears running down my cheeks, for Matthew is lying on the bed looking so white, and I'm afraid the doctor's words will come true.

"What can I do for him?" I ask. "How could I have been so stupid as to let him eat those berries!"

When Dr. Skill sees how frightened I am, he speaks gently. "Don't be too unhappy, Christiana. I have some of the King's medicine with me. If Matthew didn't eat too much fruit, it will do him good."

CHAPTER 17
Dr. Skill

Dr. Skill prepares some pills and tries to get Matthew to swallow them. But Matthew refuses, even though he's groaning with stomach pain and saying he feels as though he's being pulled to pieces inside.

"Come on," the doctor says, "you have to take them."

Still Matthew refuses.

"Matthew, do as the doctor tells you," I say firmly.

"I'll be sick," Matthew says. "Then they'll all come up again."

Maybe he has a point, so I pick up one of the pills and touch it on my tongue, warily. It tastes slightly of honey, but has no strong flavor. "Matthew," I say firmly, "if you love me, and if you love your brothers, and if you love Mercy and love your own life, *take your medicine!*"

I know I sound rather strict, but it works. Matthew sits up and swallows the pills. Almost immediately he breaks out in a sweat and has to rush to the bathroom. He comes back rather

Part 2 - Christiana's Story

embarrassed, but he's already looking better, and walks around the bedroom holding onto my arm, and smiling.

Matthew is so excited to be feeling better, that he goes off to tell Prudence, Piety and Charity how he's been healed.

"I'd like to keep some of those pills with me," I tell Dr. Skill, and he's willing to prepare some and tell me how and when to use them. It seems they will heal almost any sickness in a true pilgrim.

I decide it was probably a good thing for Matthew that he suffered so much, for he now seems more ready to listen to my advice. He even agrees to let Prudence teach him, and comes to her as my other brothers did, asking her to explain things he doesn't understand about the King and his Son.

The time passes pleasantly, and toward the end of the month Joseph reminds me that we want Greatheart to guide us on our way to the Celestial City.

"He was so good to us, and he's so brave," my brother says. "How can we find out if Interpreter will let him come?"

"I will write to him," I say.

So I write a letter and give it to Watchful, who sends it with a messenger to the house of Interpreter. In the evening the messenger returns, saying that Interpreter is sending Greatheart to guide us further on our journey.

Prudence and her sisters tell us they're sorry to let us leave, and once again they show us the treasures for which the House Beautiful is so famous. There's a small golden anchor on a neck chain in one of the rooms, and every time I see it, I admire it.

"You can have it for yourself, if you like," Piety tells me. "Wear it, and when you look at it, don't forget what it means."

"What *does* it mean?" I ask, for I've never liked to ask before.

"You know the purpose of an anchor, I'm sure," Prudence says. "When it is securely on the seabed a strong anchor holds their ship safely away from the rocks, even though the waves may be high and the wind roaring all around them. So if you love the King, trust him to help you no matter what is happening in your life, and that trust will be like an anchor for you. Even when you're in the greatest danger or difficulty, you need never be afraid."

Prudence fastens the chain round my neck, and I say, "Thank you ever so much. I'm so glad to have it, for it will help me remember all you've taught us."

We hear a knock at the door, and Watchful sends word that Greatheart has arrived. Joseph and James run to cling on to him.

"I have brought you a gift," Greatheart tells me, and I'm pleased to see he's still wearing his armor. He shows me a large pack containing fruit and some bottles that he explains are from Interpreter. "It will be easy for me to carry," he says, "and you'll need it whenever we're not able to find anywhere to stop and get food."

Part 2 - Christiana's Story

CHAPTER 18
The Dark Valley

I'm pleased at Interpreter's kindness in sending not only Greatheart, but some food for our journey. I thank Prudence and her sisters for making our stay at the House Beautiful so pleasant. Even though it's early, we are ready to leave.

"We'll walk to the bottom of the hill with you," Prudence tells us. "The path can be slippery and rather dangerous, and we want to make sure you all get down safely."

As we pass through the gates I say goodbye to Watchful, and ask him if any other pilgrims have gone by recently.

Watchful says, "No, but a man stayed with me in my lodge last night, and he told me that some pilgrims have recently been attacked and robbed by the evil prince's servants on the road ahead."

We all stop, looking around as though the thieves are hiding in the bushes.

"There's no need to worry," Watchful assures us. "Our King's soldiers heard about it and caught the men, and now they're in prison."

Mercy turns pale, but Matthew touches her hand and whispers, "You needn't be afraid, Mercy. We have Greatheart with us."

I'm so pleased to see Matthew not only well, but more caring than he has been. I can hear something singing in the trees nearby.

> "Through all my life Thy favor is
> So frankly show'd to me,
> That in Thy house for evermore
> My dwelling-place shall be."

I listen carefully, puzzled. Another voice now answers the first.

> "For why? The Lord our God is good,
> His mercy is forever sure;
> His truth at all times firmly stood,
> And shall from age to age endure."

I ask Prudence what it is that's singing. "They're our country birds," she says. "They especially like to sing in the spring, when the flowers appear and the sun shines warmly. Then they sing all day long. I often go out to hear them, and sometimes they live in our house as tame birds. They're good company when we're feeling sad. They make the woods and lonely places pleasant to be in."

Part 2 - Christiana's Story

The singing has stopped now, and I'm glad I was close enough to hear it. We begin to descend the steep path that leads into the Dark Valley. It's slippery, as Prudence warned us it would be, but we reach the valley in safety.

Piety tells us, "Soon you will pass the place where Christian fought the Destroyer. But if he comes out to meet you, you mustn't be alarmed. Greatheart will take good care of you, and the King is always ready to help."

We follow Greatheart down the valley, as the three sisters return to the House Beautiful. This is a lovely spot, and sweet-scented lilies cover the ground. This certainly can't be the Dark Valley.

"I can't think the evil prince or his servants ever come here," I tell Greatheart. "It's all so peaceful."

"This part of the valley is the favorite of our King's Son," Greatheart says. "He lived here for a time. But you mustn't expect to find anywhere the evil prince and his servants don't come – not until you're in the King's City. But soon we will be entering the part that is called the Dark Valley, and you will see why it got its name."

Presently James points to some sheep, with lambs skipping happily around them. A boy is taking care of the sheep, but he's among the trees and hasn't seen us, although we can see him. He's singing to himself.

"He's poor," Greatheart explains, "yet he's happy. He works hard and knows his Master is pleased with him. The King has given him these sheep to care for, and he looks for nothing more than to work faithfully for his Master."

236

Greatheart now warns us that we are entering the Dark Valley. He tells us Christian had to pass through it alone. It's now early in the afternoon, and Greatheart says he hopes he'll be able to guide us safely through the worst part before dark.

I imagine it's always gloomy in the Dark Valley, for the high rocks on each side lean towards each other, stopping the sunlight reaching the path below. Greatheart is looking closely at us. Mercy holds my hand, and her lips are trembling, so I point to the anchor I'm wearing. There could well be a stormy time ahead, and I think she realizes why I'm showing it to her. Our trust in the King and his Son will be like an anchor keeping us in safety.

Greatheart smiles. "I can see you're both thinking of the King," he says.

Joseph and James don't look nearly as calm as I feel, and I'm sorry for them. We hear strange noises among the rocks, and the noises, and the dimness of the light, seem to frighten them more than the sight of the dangerous pathway. Suddenly the ground shakes under our feet, and we hear a loud hissing noise like angry snakes.

"Are we nearly through yet?" James asks.

"Not yet," is all Greatheart says. Maybe he doesn't want to worry us by telling us what's ahead.

Matthew asks Joseph to walk with him, and James keeps close to Samuel. Both older brothers are obviously doing their best to cheer and encourage the younger two.

"Follow me carefully," Greatheart tells us, "and keep alert or you'll miss your footing. Remember, if you trust in the King and his Son, the evil prince and his servants can do nothing to harm you."

James suddenly trips, and Samuel catches him with his hands. Greatheart steps back, and stooping down, lifts James up.

I look anxiously into James' face. I'm afraid someone has hurt him.

"He's only tired," Greatheart tells me. "If you give him some of Dr. Skill's medicine he'll soon revive."

I manage to persuade James to swallow three pills with a little water, and he opens his eyes and says he's already feeling better.

"I was frightened," he says. "I thought I saw some horrible things. Will the King be angry with me?"

"No," Greatheart tells him, "he knows what this valley is like."

"Where did the Destroyer meet Christian?" James asks. "Are we going to go past the place?"

"We're coming to it soon," Greatheart says. "The Destroyer is the King's enemy, and he often meets pilgrims in this part of the Dark Valley. It's called Forgetful Green."

"Why?" Samuel asks. He's certainly the one who wants to know everything.

Before Greatheart can answer, a terrifying creature rushes out from behind a rock. I know it's Apollyon, the Destroyer. Greatheart raises his sword and orders him to leave us alone – in the King's name. The sword seems to have special powers from the King. Suddenly the Destroyer is gone.

Greatheart is looking around, keeping an eye open for more danger. "There's a lesson to learn here," he says. "The King says that if we resist evil in his name, it will flee from us."

We all feel relieved to hear that. Samuel asks how the Dark Valley got its name. I look into the gloom and think the answer is obvious. But Greatheart tells us more than the obvious.

"It got its name because when pilgrims have been staying at the House Beautiful, they often forget that the Way of the King is not all smooth and easy," he explains. "They begin to think that the dangers are past, and suddenly they have a bad fall on their way down the hill. Then they enter into a time of darkness."

"Did Christian fall?" Mercy asks.

Greatheart nods. "He did, several times, and that's when the Destroyer attacks pilgrims. But Christian loved the King and wouldn't let the Destroyer persuade him to turn round and give up his journey."

We reach the place where the battle took place, and Greatheart tells the story over again. All the boys are now asking questions, and I'm pleased to know they love to hear of Christian's bravery, and how the King helped him to overcome his enemy.

Greatheart shows us the rock where Christian rested after the battle, and Joseph shouts that he can see some dried blood on the stones. He wonders if it's Christian's. I don't like to look, but feel happier when Greatheart tells us that Christian dreamt that the King's Son was with him, rubbing his wounds with healing leaves. When he woke up, he was healed.

Part 2 - Christiana's Story

CHAPTER 19
Another Lion

The Dark Valley is a terrible place. I keep imagining I can see strange shapes among the shadows. But Greatheart keeps going steadily forward, and we follow him closely until he tells us we're about halfway through.

Mercy turns round and shouts that she can see a lion coming after us. It roars as it draws near. Greatheart orders us to go ahead while he waits for the savage beast. When the creature realizes that its enemy is prepared to fight instead of running away, it crouches down on the path and comes no closer.

Greatheart goes back into the lead. Suddenly he stops, holding up his hand. "Stay where you are," he calls. "The path has broken away. If we go on, we may fall into a deep pit."

Matthew makes his way cautiously to the front. "I think I can get past," he says.

"And what about your brothers?" Greatheart asks.

I'm about to say it might be possible for all of us to continue, when a thick mist rises up around us so can't even see each other.

"This is dreadful," I cry out. "Now what are we going to do?"

"We must call to the King's Son," Greatheart says, sounding bold. "He's here, although we can't see him, and he won't leave us. That pit may not be real. The evil prince has power in this valley to make us imagine dangers that are not really there. Stand still, everybody, until the mist clears away."

We keep hold of each other's hands, calling aloud to the King's Son to deliver us.

"It must have been worse for poor Christian than it is for us," I tell Greatheart. "He was traveling through here alone."

"Not alone," Greatheart says. "The King's Son was with him. I have brought many pilgrims along this path, and sometimes the danger has been far greater than this. The King's Son has always helped us, and we've been brought out safely."

I find Greatheart's words comforting and we wait patiently, although the strange noises and the sound of footsteps hurrying up and down are terrifying in the thick mist. But no one comes near to hurt us, and after a time a light begins to break through the heavy mist. It's clear enough now to see the ground.

"It is as I suspected," Greatheart tells us. "The pathway wasn't broken at all, and there is no deep pit. The evil prince was trying to deceive us."

Part 2 - Christiana's Story

We're so thankful, and gladly go on our way. But a horrible smell begins to fill the valley making us choke, so that the air is hardly fit to breathe.

"This is a bad part of our pilgrimage," Mercy sighs. "I loved it at the Wicket Gate, and at Interpreter's house and at the House Beautiful."

"I know," Samuel says, sounding surprisingly wise, "but think how much worse it would be to live here all the time, as we might be forced to do if we served the evil prince. Perhaps the King wants us to pass through this dark place so we can appreciate the light and other good things better, and then want to help other people who are in darkness."

"You are very observant, Samuel" Greatheart says. "That is exactly the reason."

"Does that mean we're getting to the end of the valley?" Joseph asks hopefully. "My feet are tired with walking on this narrow path."

"We're almost through," Greatheart promises, "but now you must be even more careful, because we're coming to the traps."

CHAPTER 20
Traps

"Traps?" Joseph and James ask together. "What traps?"

Greatheart looks serious. "When Christian passed this way, he found the ground near the end of the Dark Valley was covered with traps and snares on the ground to catch pilgrims."

Greatheart leads us along slowly, but I find it difficult to walk on this dangerous path without falling, or getting my feet tangled in wires. We see a man lying by the side of the path.

"His name is Heedless," Greatheart tells us. "He thought he could walk safely without any help from the King. But as he hurried along, his feet became caught in a snare that threw him down. His companion, who was called Take-Heed, couldn't unfasten it, no matter how hard he tried."

"Did Take-Heed escape?" Mercy asks.

"He did, but he had to leave his friend in the power of the evil prince."

I want to move Heedless, but Greatheart assures us many pilgrims have tried before. Heedless wants to stay where he is, and refuses help.

Part 2 - Christiana's Story

We reach the end of the valley and Greatheart points to a cave. "A giant lives in there," he says. "His name is Maul. He knows me and he hates me. Whenever I bring pilgrims out of the valley, he tries to stop us. His name means that ~~means that~~ he hurts people by knocking them about."

We draw near the cave, and Maul's massive head looks out. Seeing us, he waves a large club and shouts angrily, "How often have you been forbidden to do these things, Greatheart?"

"To do what things?" Greatheart asks.

"What things? What things? You know exactly what I mean," Giant Maul roars, "and I'm putting a stop to it." He seizes his great club, and lumbers down the rocky path towards us.

"Tell me why you're attacking me," Greatheart says quietly.

"Because you're a kidnapper," the giant shouts.

"Can you be more precise?" Greatheart calls back.

"I can tell you exactly what you do," the giant shouts in anger. "You catch men, women and children, and lead them to a strange country far away from my master's kingdom."

"I am a servant of the King," Greatheart calls. "It is my duty to help people to turn to the King, to take them from the darkness of your master's kingdom into the light. If you want to fight me because I obey the King, I'm ready for you."

Giant Maul rushes at Greatheart, and strikes him such a terrible blow with his club that Greatheart falls on his knees. I scream in fright, for I think our faithful guide is about to be killed. But Greatheart springs up and rips the giant's arm with his sword.

The two fight fiercely for what seems like an hour, and the breath comes out of the giant's nostrils like steam from a boiling kettle.

At last the giant stops fighting, but he still refuses to let us go past. He sits down on a large rock to rest, and Greatheart turns away and calls to the King to give him new strength to win the battle. I'm sorry to say the rest of us do absolutely nothing to help.

Giant Maul jumps up, looking ready to fight more fiercely than before. "I'm going to kill you, Greatheart," he roars. "Then I'm going to take these pilgrims back to my prince, and get a big reward."

Part 2 - Christiana's Story

CHAPTER 21
Giant Maul

I know deep down that the King won't leave Greatheart to fight on his own. When the fight begins again, I can see Greatheart's strength and courage increasing every moment, and before long he knocks the giant to the ground.

Maul cries for pity, and Greatheart allows him to get up. But it's a trick, and as Maul clambers to his feet he strikes at the young soldier with his club. The blow crashes down on Greatheart's head, and if Greatheart's helmet wasn't so strong he'd be dead.

But I can see that Maul's power is failing, and he can no longer hold his heavy club. As it falls from his hands, Greatheart thrusts his sword through the giant's chest. In a few moments Greatheart stands alone on the pathway, the giant dead at his feet.

Greatheart raises his sword and cuts off the giant's head with a single blow. We start to cheer, for although the fight was terrifying to see, we know the giant was one of the King's terrible enemies, and it's right for Greatheart to destroy him.

Near the giant's cave we find some large stones. The boys roll them down to the pathway and help Greatheart build a pillar. With great excitement they haul the head of the giant onto the top.

Greatheart writes a notice, and fastens it on a post where it will be easy to read.

> *He that did wear this head, was one*
> *That pilgrims did misuse;*
> *He stopped their way, he spared none,*
> *But did them all abuse;*
> *Until that I, Greatheart, arose,*
> *The pilgrim's guide to be;*
> *Until that I did him oppose,*
> *That was their enemy.*

"Now everyone will know the giant is dead," James says, wiping his hands on the grass. "Wasn't Greatheart brave?"

He certainly was. I look once more at Giant Maul's head on top of the pillar, and shudder. I try to imagine Matthew and Samuel with swords, fighting giants. Well, if Christian could do it, surely they can. Maybe I could fight a giant – if I had one of the King's swords.

A little distance from the cave we reach a small hill. Greatheart tells us it's time to take a rest, and see what lies ahead. As we sit comfortably on the grass, I turn to Greatheart. "Were you frightened when the giant hit you with his club?" I ask.

Part 2 - Christiana's Story

Greatheart smiles. "At times, but I knew the King would help me, because I was only doing my duty. The King's Son was once wounded, but he conquered in the end, and he won't let his servants be defeated if we're faithful to him."

I can see some huge bruises on Greatheart's arms. I ask him if he's badly hurt.

"Not badly," he says. "My armor is so good that I only have a few cuts and bruises, and they'll soon heal. And any that don't heal will remind me that I received them fighting for the King."

It is now late in the evening, and although it's summer, the light is already beginning to fade. From the hill we see an old man sitting on the ground under an oak tree. He's holding a staff in his hand, but his eyes are closed and he seems to be asleep.

"He might be a pilgrim," Matthew says as we get close. "He's certainly dressed like one."

"Yes," Greatheart tells him, "I recognize this man, and we mustn't leave him here."

He touches the old man's shoulder to wake him up, and he springs up trembling. Perhaps he thinks the enemy is trying to capture him.

"What's the matter?" the old man cries in fright. "Who are you, and what is your business here?"

CHAPTER 22
Mr. Honest

Greatheart says he's sorry he startled the man. "You needn't be afraid of us," he tells him. "We're all friends."

But the old pilgrim isn't satisfied. He looks anxiously at Greatheart and then at Matthew, and asks again who we are.

Greatheart stands back a little to give the old man room to move. "My name is Greatheart, and I'm taking these pilgrims to the Celestial City."

The man smiles. "I thought you were robbers," he says, laughing, "but I can see now that you're the King's servants."

"What would you have done if we *had* been robbers?" I ask, for the elderly pilgrim doesn't look fit enough to defend himself.

"I know I'm only a feeble old man," he says, "but I would have called to the King, and then I would have fought. Yes, I would have fought as long as I had any breath, and I don't think *anyone* would have overcome me."

"You speak like a good pilgrim," Greatheart tells him. "Will you tell us your name?"

Part 2 - Christiana's Story

The old man shakes his head. "Never mind my name. I'm only a poor fellow. I used to live in a place called Stupidity, a few miles from the City of Destruction."

Greatheart looks at the old man. "I am always surprised when I hear of any pilgrim coming from your town, for it's even worse than City of Destruction," he says. Suddenly he smiles and goes forward and seizes the man by the hand. "I think I know you. Are you Mr. Honesty?"

"Not quite," the man says. "My name is Mr. Honest, but it's only by the help of the King that I can be true to it. How do you know anything about me?"

Greatheart smiles. "I have heard the King's Son speaking well of you," he says.

The old pilgrim's face flushes all over with pleasure, for it's obvious that he loves the King's Son with his whole heart.

Mr. Honest is friendly, and he has a kind, good-natured face. It's nearly dark now, and Greatheart is talking to Mr. Honest about his pilgrimage, and we're all listening. Greatheart asks Mr. Honest if he remembers one of his old friends named Fearing.

"Yes, indeed," Mr. Honest says. "I've often thought about him. We used to live near each other. He was a pilgrim too. Has Fearing reached the Celestial City safely?"

"My Master sent me with him," Greatheart explains. "He was one of the most troublesome pilgrims I ever met in all my days. He was always afraid. Although he loved the King, he thought he would be turned away from the Gates of the Celestial City when he got there. He fancied he was too weak and poor for the King to notice him. He told me he had stayed for nearly a month by the edge of the Slough of Despond, because he felt sure he would sink in if he tried to get across. Many people offered to help him over, but although he watched them cross safely, he wouldn't try for himself."

"But he must have crossed in the end," Mercy says, "or you wouldn't have been able to help him."

"Oh yes, after a long time," Greatheart agrees. "One bright morning he took courage, and when he reached the firm ground beyond the Slough he could scarcely believe the danger was really past. Then at the Wicket Gate he behaved in the same way. He didn't think he would be allowed through, so he wouldn't knock, he was so chicken-hearted. Other pilgrims came to the Wicket Gate, and Goodwill let them in, but Fearing drew back so that Goodwill never saw him. At last he crept up to the Wicket Gate and gave one timid knock. Goodwill came at once and let Fearing in, but he was afraid to show his face because he said he wasn't good enough."

"I know how he felt," Mercy says, blushing. "I was like Fearing when I entered the Way of the King."

"I think many people approach the Wicket Gate with doubts," Mr. Honest tells us. "But what happened to Fearing?"

Part 2 - Christiana's Story

CHAPTER 23
Fearing

Greatheart tells us that Goodwill wrote a letter for Fearing to take to Interpreter, asking him to send a guide to go with poor Fearing all the way to the Celestial City. But Fearing spent several days and nights in the cold outside Interpreter's gates before anyone knew he was there. Then one morning Greatheart happened to see him from one of the windows, and went down to speak to him. Fearing was weak for want of food, but he brought out Goodwill's letter, and after a little trouble Greatheart persuaded him to enter the house.

"And did you stay with Fearing all the way after that?" Mr. Honest asks.

Greatheart nods. "All the way. Fearing was pleased when we came to the Cross, and stayed there a long time lost in thought. Whatever he was thinking, it seemed to cheer him up. He didn't mind Hill Difficulty, or the lions each side of the path. He wasn't afraid of such things. He was only afraid the King would think he wasn't fit to be a pilgrim."

"Did Fearing stay at the House Beautiful?" I ask. I have many happy memories of that place.

"Fearing loved it there," Greatheart says. "He was too shy to have much to do with the four sisters, or with their other guests, but he liked to sit in the corner and listen to them talking. We stayed a long time in the pleasant valley below the house, for my Master told me not to hurry him. He seemed to love the sweet-scented lilies and other flowers so much that he couldn't bear to leave the place."

Mr. Honest looks pleased to hear that. "But how did he get on when you reached the Dark Valley?" he asks.

"I was afraid it would be terrible for him," Greatheart says. "And indeed it was, but the King didn't allow him to be troubled in the way many pilgrims are. I never saw the valley so light or so quiet at any other time. In Vanity Fair he was angry at the wickedness he saw around him, but he was braver there than anywhere, and was ready to fight the enemies of the King at every turn. However, we passed through the town without being hurt, and after traveling slowly for some time we came to the Dark River in the Land of Beulah."

"Fearing must have been happy when he saw the Gates of the Celestial City," Mr. Honest says.

Greatheart shakes his head. "Not at first. He wandered along the river bank, looking across at the bright walls, and saying that he was sure the King would never receive him. He kept saying he'd be lost in the deep water. But when the message came for him to go across, I went down to watch. The water was so low that he went over easily. Then the angels met him on the other side, and I saw him no more."

Mr. Honest is glad to hear of his old friend's pilgrimage, and to know he reached the Celestial City safely.

I say, "I thought I was the only person who's afraid that perhaps the King won't receive them. I feel afraid so often."

"So do I," Mercy whispers.

"And I do," Matthew admits. "And then I think maybe the King will be angry with me for even thinking it."

"No," Greatheart assures us, "he won't be displeased. I think all good pilgrims feel anxious sometimes."

Mr. Honest turns and looks at each one of us. "If anyone imagines they're good enough to be admitted to the Celestial City, it shows they aren't the King's true servants," he says in a gentle voice. "No pilgrim can reach the Celestial City by trying to be good enough. The King will only let us in because of his Son. I once traveled with a pilgrim whose name was Self-Will. He never troubled himself at all about King. He thought he only needed to do his best to follow the path until he came to the City, and he would *surely* be received there. But he was wrong."

While Mr. Honest is talking, a man passes by and says to Greatheart, "You must be careful, there's a gang of trouble makers out tonight."

Greatheart thanks the man for the warning, and asks Matthew to help keep watch as we go along. Matthew seems to have grown up so much since we started, and he's much taller than me now. But we meet no one, and I wonder if the gang have heard that Greatheart is coming and are hiding away in fright. Or maybe they're off somewhere else causing trouble.

Part 2 - Christiana's Story

CHAPTER 24
Gaius

My two youngest brothers are complaining that they're feeling tired after their long day, and I have to admit I'm exhausted. The sun has already set, and I keep thinking of the two giants Greatheart has killed – Giant Grim and Giant Maul. We've had enough excitement for one day, and it's time to find somewhere to sleep for the night – preferably indoors. I ask Greatheart if he knows of a place where we can rest in safety.

"A friend of mine keeps an inn near here," Mr. Honest says. "His name is Gaius. We'll soon see his place, and I'm sure he'll let us stay the night."

The inn is only a short distance away, and Gaius makes us comfortable. He tells us he always welcomes pilgrims to his inn, and his servants are pleased to have the opportunity to shelter us. While the cook is preparing supper, Gaius invites us to sit down and rest. He has much to say to Greatheart and his old friend Mr. Honest, and we listen quietly and feel at ease.

Presently a servant comes in, spreads a cloth on the table, and lays out plates and bread. The cook sends up the supper, and we're really thankful to see the good food placed before us – meat and potatoes, milk, butter and honey, and a dish of large red apples and other fruit.

When Matthew sees the fruit, I think he remembers the poison berries that made him so ill when we were at the House Beautiful.

"Is it all right to eat it?" he asks, looking embarrassed.

"Oh, yes," Gaius tells him, "this is wholesome fruit."

Matthew explains why he is afraid.

"But those were poisoned berries growing in the garden of the evil prince," Gaius says. "*This* fruit is from the King's orchards, and will hurt no one."

After supper, Gaius gives my brothers some nuts to crack, and while they eat them he goes on talking to Greatheart.

Samuel picks up one of the nuts and laughs. "I think we've been given these to teach us a lesson," he says.

I look at him in astonishment. "What lesson?" I ask, loudly enough to catch the attention of Gaius.

Samuel cracks the shell and eats the nut. "These nuts are like some of the readings in the King's Book," he says. "The outside is hard to crack, but if we try hard enough we can get to the good food inside."

He sits back looking more than a little pleased with himself, and Gaius claps his hands. "Well said, Samuel," he calls. "That is indeed a good lesson to go to bed with. And speaking of bed . . ." He turns to Joseph and James, "I think this would be a good time for you boys to go up for the night."

Part 2 - Christiana's Story

Old Mr. Honest raises a hand. "Just a moment," he says. "The boys have cracked some nuts, but let me see if they can crack this riddle:
> "A man there was
> Though some did count him mad,
> The more he cast away,
> The more he had."

We all think hard what the man could have thrown away, and in the end we have to give up. Mr. Honest laughs and says:
> "He that bestows his goods
> Upon the poor,
> Shall have as much again,
> And ten times more."

"That's good," Joseph says. "I don't we'd ever have got it."

Gaius shows us the rooms that are ready for us: one for Mercy and me, and one for the boys. I look at Mercy and we agree it's time for all of us to retire for the night. Mr. Honest says he's so pleased to see his friend Gaius again that he'll sit by the fire – and probably talk until the sun rises in the morning. But they invite me down to talk for a few minutes while the others are getting ready for bed.

I wonder what they're going to tell me, and I feel a little anxious that one of us may have done something wrong and caused offense.

"Matthew is a fine lad," Gaius says. "I think he and Mercy are already good friends."

I'm not sure what he means. I know Matthew has grown up a lot since we started out, but surely . . .

"One day," Gaius continues, "I believe they will make a fine married couple."

I put the back of my hand to my mouth and gasp. "I've never even thought of anything like that," I say.

Gaius shakes his head and laughs gently. "I am thinking some years into the future, Christiana. However, I'm surprised you never noticed how close they are. Sometimes we don't see the obvious with our own family. But this is not the time for you to say anything to them."

It certainly isn't. I try to imagine Matthew's reaction. He would be so self-conscious that he'd probably never speak to Mercy again. And Mercy would probably be equally embarrassed, and never talk to *me* again. But I'm starting to see what Gaius means. They both love the King, and are becoming stronger pilgrims by the day.

I decide to slip from the room before getting more deeply involved, and politely say goodnight, and promise not to say anything – a promise I can easily keep! Before long I'm in bed, listening to Mercy breathing slowly in her sleep. I thank the King for bringing us here safely, and close my eyes in my comfortable bed. But I can't get to sleep. I keep thinking about Matthew and Mercy being married, wondering if it will ever be.

* * *

At breakfast, Gaius tells us about an evil giant named Slay-Good who has come to live in the hills about a mile from his house.

Part 2 - Christiana's Story

"He's strong and he's fierce," Gaius says, "but if we go to attack him, I'm sure the King will help us and give us the strength to destroy him. I've heard that the giant caught a pilgrim yesterday, and if we hurry we may be able to rescue him."

Greatheart says I can go with them, and so can Matthew, Samuel and Mercy, but the two younger boys must stay behind. They're not too happy about that. Mr. Honest says he'll go as well, for although he's old he says he likes to see the King's enemies defeated.

We reach the cave but there's no sign of the giant. Greatheart calls out loudly when we come close, and the huge giant immediately leaps out of his cave.

The battle lasts for an hour, but Slay-Good is wounded at last and falls to the ground. Greatheart stands over him while Gaius searches the cave to see if the pilgrim the giant has captured is still alive.

To everyone's relief Greatheart carries a young man out of the darkness into the daylight. "I'm so glad to see you," the man says. "My name is Feeble-Mind."

Greatheart has some food for the man, and when he has eaten and rested a little, Feeble-Mind is able to tell his story. I wonder how he got his name, for he's as bright as the rest of us. So there's certainly nothing wrong with his mind. Feeble-Mind tells us he got his name because he has never been bold, and is afraid of every difficulty he comes to. What he means, I think, is that his mind keeps telling him to do nothing. I'm surprised to find such a person taking this long journey as a pilgrim.

"But," Feeble-Mind says, "in the end I made up my mind to find the King's City, when I realized he was calling me because he wanted me. Everybody has been good to me, and I've come this far in safety. I would have been too worried about climbing Hill Difficulty on my own, but Interpreter sent someone with me and he carried me on his back to the top of the rocky path. Being caught by the giant last night is the worst thing that has happened to me so far, but as I lay in the cave I called to the King. I felt sure he would save me – and as you can see, he did."

The giant roars with terror as Greatheart raises his sharp sword. But Greatheart shows no mercy. He cuts the giant's head off with a single stroke. Cutting the heads off giants seems to be the standard course of action for Greatheart, and he drags Slay-Good's head back to the inn by the hair so everyone can see it and be glad that another of the King's enemies is dead.

James keeps complaining he should have been there to watch Greatheart do it. "With a single stroke of the sword," he says, wielding an imaginary weapon high above his head, then swinging it down to the ground. "Take that, Giant Slay-Good!"

Part 2 - Christiana's Story

CHAPTER 25
Off Again

Gaius has a young daughter whose name is Phoebe. She tells us she has already passed through the Wicket Gate, and now wants to go to the Celestial City. Her father says it would be good for her to travel with us. Phoebe looks almost too small to travel, although she must be about the same age as James. But she insists on going with us, so Gaius asks us to stay for a few days while his daughter prepares for her journey.

On the last day Gaius makes a feast for us, and when it's over Greatheart asks what he must pay for our lodging. But Gaius refuses to take any money. He says he loves the King and his Son, and for the King's sake he keeps his inn ready for any pilgrims who chose to stay here.

We're saying goodbye, and Feeble-Mind stands silently in the doorway. Greatheart says to him, "Aren't you coming with us? The King will be glad for us to help you on your way."

Feeble-Mind shakes his head. "I'm afraid I'll slow you down," he explains. "You are all so strong and active, and I'm so nervous of everything. Besides, I'm not cheerful like these young pilgrims, and I think I'd make them feel sad with my dull ways."

"Oh no, you won't," I tell him. "Come with us, and we'll cheer you up and help you."

"Yes," Greatheart insists, "it's dangerous to travel alone. We'll be sorry if we have to leave you behind."

I can see tears come into the poor man's eyes, but we can't persuade Feeble-Mind to travel with us. I think he really *is* afraid of slowing us down. While we're standing together on the pathway, we hear footsteps approaching slowly and hesitantly, and a young pilgrim comes in sight. He says his name is Ready-to-Halt. He's probably Matthew's age, and has to walk with the aid of crutches.

When Feeble-Mind sees him, he exclaims, "I know you! How did you get here?"

The boy smiles as he holds out his hand. "Feeble-Mind! How did *you* get here?" he asks. "I do believe we're both bound for the same place."

"You're disabled, and I'm weak," I hear Feeble-Mind say, "but I know the King won't turn us away from the Gates of his City. I was just wishing for a companion, and no one could suit me better than you."

"I'll be only too glad to go with you," Ready-to-Halt tells him, looking round at everybody. "Can we all go together?"

Greatheart says that will be fine, and everything is settled.

Ready-to-Halt shows his crutches to us. "These are like the King's promises," he says. "Whenever I'm unsteady, I use them to keep me from falling."

Greatheart says that's something we can all do with. "Anyway," he adds, "we won't be traveling fast. So if you're not able to keep up with us, we'll always wait for you."

We set off once more. Mr. Honest walks in front with Greatheart, while Matthew and his three brothers follow. I'm walking with Mercy and Phoebe, and last of all come the Ready-to-Halt and Feeble-Mind.

"I'm sure we'll be able to help each other," I hear Ready-to-Halt say to Feeble-Mind, "and when you're tired I can lend you one of my crutches."

CHAPTER 26
Near Vanity Fair

We spend the day crossing the plain, a flat, wild area where nothing much grows. After walking for several hours, we see the walls and gates of Vanity Fair in the distance. The great towers rise darkly against the clear sky, and I begin to feel afraid as we get nearer the town of the evil prince.

"Is this where poor Faithful died?" Mercy asks me.

Phoebe is talking to James, but she hears us. "Yes," she pipes up. "It's where the people killed Faithful, and kept Christian shut in a cage."

Mercy gasps and puts her hand to her mouth. "Do you think they'll put *us* in a cage?"

It's something I've not even considered before. I'm sure I can feel my face going white, for although Phoebe is small she sounds as though she knows what she's talking about. I try to sound calm. "If we get separated from each other, let's remember how good the King's Son has been to us. We know he's always watching over us. If we have to suffer, we must be brave because we love him."

Part 2 - Christiana's Story

Feeble-Mind and Ready-to-Halt are walking just behind us, and must have heard me too.

"Are you afraid?" Feeble-Mind asks Ready-to-Halt.

"I think we all are," I say, turning round.

"Do we *have* to pass through the town?" Mercy asks. "Isn't there a way round?"

Greatheart looks kindly at her. "We *could* go round," he says, "but then we might not find our way onto the right path again."

"I think we should go straight into the town," Phoebe says firmly, and although she's the smallest in the group, she already seems to have taken charge. "My father says the evil prince has told them to be more pleasant to pilgrims now, so they'll want to stay there forever."

Greatheart and Mr. Honest are waiting for everyone to catch up. "We'll have to spend the night in Vanity Fair," Greatheart tells us. "If we pass straight through the town we won't be able to reach another resting place before dark."

"Where can we sleep?" I ask, trying not to sound too frightened. "Will the people harm us?"

"I don't think so," Greatheart says. "I've brought many pilgrims safely through the town, and I know a good man called Mnason who keeps an inn. He will let us stay with him, and be pleased to see us, I'm sure. What do you think?"

One by one we all agree to take Greatheart's advice.

"Why would good people want to live in Vanity Fair?" Samuel asks. "Isn't it wrong for them to live there?"

Greatheart shakes his head. "The King has given them work to do. They help and protect the pilgrims who are passing through, and do their best to make sure no one decides to stay."

Part 2 - Christiana's Story

CHAPTER 27
In the Fair

The town is less busy than I expected, probably because it's now early evening. Some of the people laugh as we pass them, but other than that, no one seems interested in us. We reach the marketplace, where Greatheart shows us the spot where Faithful was killed, and soon stop at the door of a small inn.

Greatheart calls Mnason's name and a man comes out and makes us welcome.

"I thought I recognized your voice," Mnason tells Greatheart. "How far have you all traveled today?"

"From the house of our friend Gaius," Greatheart tells him.

Mnason looks surprised. "From the house of Gaius?" he says. "Well, you've certainly done a fair stitch. You must be weary, so bring your friends in and have something to eat."

Mnason shows us to a large room set with tables. As soon as we're sitting down, Mr. Honest asks Mnason if there are many good people in the town.

"We have a few," Mnason says. "But not nearly as many as there are people who are friends of the evil prince."

"Can we see some of these good folk?" Mr. Honesty asks. "To meet them is like a sailor seeing the moon and the stars instead of fog."

Mnason smiles at the expression, and signals to his young daughter called Grace. "Go and tell my friends that I have some pilgrims at my house who would like to meet them here this evening."

Grace runs off and soon comes back with a group of people. Grace has a younger sister called Martha, who is the same age as Joseph. The two sisters seem to be great friends with all these visitors.

Mnason tells us that since the death of Faithful, the people in the town have generally been much kinder to pilgrims. "I think they still feel guilty for that they did," he says. "In those days we were afraid to walk the streets, but today we can show our heads. Then, the name of the King was odious, but nowadays there are parts of the town where such conversation is considered acceptable."

Mnason fetches a viola and a lute from the next room and holds them up. "Which of you can play these?" he asks us.

"Christiana can play the viola," James says quickly, before I can shake my head at him to warn him to keep quiet. It's quite a time since I last played a violin, and although the viola may look the same, it's a bit larger. Anyway, I don't think I'll be any good – especially with so many people listening. Mercy raises her hand and offers to take the lute, which looks a little like a flat guitar. So now I have to accept the viola. We whisper together about what to play, and start off.

Part 2 - Christiana's Story

At first we don't do all that well, because the instruments feel strange. But nobody laughs, not even Joseph and James. Soon we get into the mood for playing, and it all sounds good – to me, at least.

Everybody claps politely when we finish, and the talk turns to our adventures and misadventures so far. Greatheart tells how he killed Giant Grim and Giant Maul, and now Giant Slay-Good.

"Then these pilgrims must stay a while longer," Mnason says, looking at his friends. "We have a terrifying enemy outside the town. It is a dragon called False-Teaching, and we have just had news that it caught a pilgrim this evening."

"And you'd like us help rescue the pilgrim and kill the dragon?" Samuel says. "Come on, let's all go now."

I look at my brothers. Matthew quickly nods and says that he'll help, while Joseph and James look excited. Mercy and Phoebe probably feel as I do, for we all smile vaguely.

"We must wait until the morning when it's light," Greatheart says. "It will be too dangerous to go if we cannot see the way ahead."

Mnason agrees. "I'll arrange for us to have an early breakfast. It's no good going to fight a dragon on an empty stomach."

As for Mr. Honest, Feeble-Mind and the disabled boy called Ready-to-Halt, I can see they're going to need a good rest, so I doubt if they'll be attacking any dragons in the near future. But it looks as though the rest of us will.

"By the way," Mnason adds, "you might as well know. The dragon has seven heads – on seven *very* long necks!"

Part 2 - Christiana's Story

CHAPTER 28
The Seven-Headed Dragon

It's the early morning and we're standing outside Mnason's inn in the dawn light, waiting for instructions. Joseph and James are at the front, to hear what Mnason has to say. Mnason tells us that the dragon lives in a large forest close to Vanity Fair.

I'm feeling a little afraid. If the people of Vanity Fair are terrified of the dragon, what can *we* do?

"There will be no danger if you all keep close to me," Greatheart explains. "The King told me in a dream last night that we have nothing to fear – as long as we go in his name. He has even provided weapons for every one of us."

"For James as well?" I cry in alarm, as my youngest brother rubs his hands in excitement. "Isn't he too young to fight?"

"It was probably a mistake for me to leave James and Joseph behind last time," Greatheart says. "The King's swords can be used by everyone. Even the youngest pilgrim. You are all to come with us."

"Do the people who live in Vanity Fair feed it?" I wonder aloud.

Mnason hears me. "They did at first," he says. "They thought it would be fun to make friends with a dragon, but now it's grown so bold it comes into town to attack both men and women. Sometimes it seizes children and carries them away to its lair."

"Why hasn't anyone from Vanity Fair killed it?" I ask. "With a town this size, surely they could get a small army together."

"The servants of the evil prince are afraid of it," Mnason explains. "Unfortunately none of them dares so much as face this monster, and they flee when they hear it coming. We servants of the King certainly want it dead, but until Greatheart and all you pilgrims arrived yesterday, we have not been able to do anything."

* * *

We're inside the forest now, in a place where a rocky hill rises high above the trees. Suddenly Mnason raises a hand to tell us to stay where we are. Everybody stops talking. I can feel my heart beating faster.

Mnason points to the entrance to a large cave a little way up the hill. "This is the lair of False-Teaching," he whispers.

It's strange, but now I can see the cave I don't feel quite so frightened. We climb silently, higher and higher among the rocks, until we are nearly at the entrance.

We can hear someone shouting for help, and the voice seems to be coming from inside the cave. Without warning, a head on the end of a long neck darts out. Six more heads

Part 2 - Christiana's Story

follow, then the scaly green body of the dragon, so we can see all seven heads and long necks of this disgusting creature.

The dragon stands in the mouth of the cave, its heads waving around in rage. It utters seven roars that shake the hillside as it clambers over the large rocks to attack us.

False-Teaching looks mean and strong, and I know it could kill us all if we weren't armed with the King's weapons. The fight begins. While we stab at it with our swords, Greatheart climbs above the cave, unseen by the dragon.

As the beast roars its terrifying roar, Greatheart leaps down onto its back and slashes his sword across one of the long necks. Still joined to its neck, the head rolls past us dripping blood as we all jump out of the way.

Screaming with pain, the dragon rushes back into the cave. I look down at the severed head, afraid it will bite us, but it's completely still.

"There are still six heads left," James whispers, his small sword raised in his hand, ready for another battle if the dragon gets this far.

The next attack comes while Greatheart is climbing down from the rocks. The dragon is obviously expecting Greatheart to still be above, and it looks up with all six remaining heads on the end of their long necks.

Greatheart is to one side and slashes off one head, and then another. False-Teaching is wild with a mixture of rage and pain, its long necks threshing around wildly. Mnason hurries forward to kill it, but Matthew and Samuel get there first. The terrible roars suddenly stop as the last head rolls down the hill, and dragon's body collapses in the cave entrance.

Joseph and James are the first to enter the cave, and emerge almost immediately with the trapped pilgrim. We are glad to see he's unhurt, and take him back to the town to stay with Mnason until he makes a full recovery.

When Mnason's friends hear about the death of False-Teaching, they tell us they're glad about it, and even the evil prince's citizens cannot help honoring us for our bravery. We get to know many people in the town over the next few days, and try to help some who are most in need. Mercy's sewing skills come in useful, for once again she is able to organize us into making and mending clothes for the poor.

We work together to feed and clothe those who are living in poverty, but Mercy is especially hard working, Mnason says she's a fine illustration of how pilgrims should behave. Phoebe, and Mnason's two daughters Grace and Martha, set us all a good example by showing kindness to everyone, and I keep hearing people speak well of us.

At last the time comes for us to continue our journey. Mnason says Grace and Martha entered the Wicket Gate some time ago, and have been waiting for a guide to help them on the rest of their way to the Celestial City. He asks Greatheart if he will allow them to travel with us. Greatheart answers that he will be pleased to help, which is good news for me – because now the boys will no longer outnumber the girls.

Many of the King's servants come to the gates of Vanity Fair to bid us farewell, and give us some gifts for our journey. I

Part 2 - Christiana's Story

can't help thinking how good the King has been, in letting me meet people who are so kind to us. Greatheart is given a large pack to carry, but won't tell us what's in it.

"I was afraid they'd shut us in their cage," I tell Mercy as we leave.

"So was I," she says. "But we found good friends there, and the King kept us safe."

CHAPTER 29
Doubting Castle

Greatheart is telling us about the River of the Water of Life, which is only a day's journey from Vanity Fair. He says we'll be able to spend tonight in its quiet meadows, which sounds good.

We are glad to rest by the River, but Greatheart warns is that we must not stay there more than a day, or it will be hard to get going again. We bathe in its water, and set off early the next morning, a large group of travelers now.

In the middle of the day we reach a stile leading to a place called By-Path Meadow. We tell Greatheart our feet are hurting, for the road has been uneven, and ask if we can walk on the smooth path just the other side of the hedge.

"We can get through the hedge later, if things go wrong," I say. "I'm sure it will be easy to rejoin the path."

Then we notice a stone with some words cut into the smooth surface:

Part 2 - Christiana's Story

Over this stile is the way to Doubting Castle
Which is kept by Giant Despair,
Who despises the King of the Celestial Country
And seeks to destroy his holy pilgrims.
The Key of Promise opens all the giant's locks.

Greatheart says Christian and his friend Hopeful put the stone here by the side of the road. He tells us how Christian and Hopeful went to sleep in By-Path Meadow in a storm, and were captured the next morning by Giant Despair and his wife Diffidence. Of course, I feel so ashamed that I thought of leading everyone onto the wrong path.

"Why doesn't someone kill the giants?" Samuel asks, and I agree it sounds an excellent idea. I'm getting quite used to seeing giants and other monsters having their heads cut off, even if there is a lot of blood and noise.

"We're not strong enough, are we?" James says, looking at Greatheart. "But *you* could kill the *biggest* giant."

Greatheart smiles. "Only with the help of the King," he says. "And the King will help *you* if you trust in him."

"So *we* could kill Giant Despair – and his wife?" James asks in a hushed voice.

"Yes."

"Come on, let's try!" Joseph shouts eagerly. "Those giants have killed lots of pilgrims."

Matthew's eyes look surprisingly bright. "Perhaps there are some pilgrims shut up in the castle," he says. "If there are, we can rescue them."

Matthew certainly seems to have gained a lot of courage. Perhaps we've all got bolder. "But isn't it wrong to leave the Way of the King?" I ask. Yes, I've changed my tune now.

"If the boys really wish to fight with Giant Despair and his wife, and destroy their castle, the King won't be displeased," Greatheart tells me. "Christian and Hopeful went over the stile because, like you, they thought the way would be easier. That's why they fell into trouble."

"I'll go first," Matthew says. I can hardly believe the change in Matthew lately. "I helped kill the dragon called False-Teaching in the cave near Vanity Fair."

Greatheart nods. "You were all brave when we attacked the dragon. Are you ready to fight like fearless soldiers again?"

The boys are only too eager. They shout that they'll follow Greatheart to Doubting Castle, and Mr. Honest says he must certainly go with them. Feeble-Mind and Ready-to-Halt won't be able to fight, so Greatheart gives Mercy and me a sword each and tells us to stay back with the others, to protect them if the enemy comes.

I hold my sword tightly, feeling pleased that I should be given such a responsible task. I hope I won't let anyone down. Mercy smiles at me, holding her sword in the air. Well, we can certainly try our best – and of course call to the King for help.

Greatheart and his group go out of sight. It's quite late in the day when they return, dragging the heads of two giants along the path. They also have two pilgrims walking with them. One is a man with a sad and weary face, and the other a young woman. Samuel explains they've been lying in the dark

Part 2 - Christiana's Story

dungeon for six days. The man looks pale and faint, and lies on the grass while Phoebe helps me rub his cold hands. While we're doing this, Grace and Martha make sure he eats some wholesome food.

At last the man sits up and thanks us. He says his name is Despondency, and he was traveling to the Celestial City with his young daughter Much-Afraid. His daughter was doing her best to help him, but they quickly lost all hope of being rescued from Doubting Castle, and can scarcely believe they're free now.

I notice Matthew's sword still has blood on the end. Maybe he's left it on there so I can see it. "You did well to kill the giants," I say to him. "I'm proud of you." This evening Matthew looks older and stronger than ever. Come to that, we're all a lot older than when we first set out.

Matthew's eyes sparkle. "When we got to the castle we knocked as loudly we could. Giant Despair comes to the door, and he has his wife Diffidence with him." He glances at the two heads on the ground. "That's her," he says, pointing. "The one with the long hair."

"I guessed," I say.

"Well," Matthew continues, "Giant Despair demands to know who we are. So Greatheart shouts, 'It is I, Greatheart, one of the King's guides for pilgrims. I have come to cut off your heads and demolish Doubting Castle.'"

"That's exactly what he said," James says, jumping up and down. "But Giant Despair didn't seem worried. He said no one could kill him."

"He was wearing armor," Samuel explains. "He had a steel helmet and breastplate."

"And metal shoes on his feet," Joseph says.

"And a huge great club," James adds. "His wife joined in the fight, but Mr. Honest killed her with one great big poke with his sharp sword."

I look at the old man, who shrugs and smiles modestly.

"That wasn't the end of it, though," James says, waving his own sword. "We couldn't kill Giant Despair. I stuck my sword into his leg, but he didn't seem to notice." And he thrust it forward fiercely, just in case none of us understood.

"I slashed his arms and they started pouring blood, but it was Greatheart who finished him off," Matthew says, managing to get a word in at last. "We thought Giant Despair had as many lives as a cat, but we knew he was dead when Greatheart cut his head off."

I nod. "That does tend to show a giant is dead," I say dryly. "Anyway, it's all over now." And I can't say I'm sorry to have missed the fight.

Mercy stands close to Matthew and smiles at him. "You must have been fearless," she says. "I'm glad *we* didn't fall into the giant's hands." She looks across at the two pilgrims who have just been rescued. Her face grows serious. "Much-Afraid looks as if she might die even now."

I remember the pills Dr. Skill gave me, and Much-Afraid swallows them with difficulty. Soon she smiles and gets to her feet.

Part 2 - Christiana's Story

"You'll soon grow stronger if we take care of you," Greatheart tells her confidently.

"Did you destroy the castle?" I ask.

James is nearly bursting with excitement. "We busted down all the gates and doors. You should have seen us."

Matthew's eyes shine as he puts his sword back into its sheath. "That was a good fight," he says, "but Greatheart says there will be more battles on the path ahead."

Greatheart opens the large pack he's been carrying since leaving Vanity Fair, and takes out Mnason's viola and lute. He passes me the viola and gives Mercy the lute. I open my eyes wide in amazement. I had no idea what Greatheart had in that pack. The mystery is solved at last. I look at Mercy, and right from the start we are able to play a cheerful tune in harmony.

Ready-to-Halt takes Despondency's daughter, Much-Afraid, by the hand, and tries to dance with her. His crutches are in the way so he throws them to the side of the road. He can't dance properly with them, and he can't dance properly without them. Much-Afraid still hasn't regained her strength, and I'm not sure who is holding who up. But before long the two are dancing surprisingly well.

Despondency says he's more interested in eating than dancing, and I don't think he's eaten anything for days. Mercy carries on playing, while I give Despondency some of Dr. Skill's medicine and something to eat. Greatheart, meanwhile, is putting the giants' heads on two wooden posts. James asks him why he's doing it.

"To warn other pilgrims not to go near Doubting Castle," he explains.

"But the giants are dead and their doors and gates are smashed down," James says, with a puzzled frown.

"True." Greatheart pushes Despair's head down firmly onto the post. "But you can be sure that other giants will soon rebuild them, and cause just as much trouble as these two."

Part 2 - Christiana's Story

CHAPTER 30
The Shepherds

Now that Greatheart and the boys have rescued the two pilgrims from Doubting Castle, there are even more of us traveling together. Mr. Honest has taken charge of Despondency, and we girls say we'll look after his young daughter, Much-Afraid.

"We're coming to the Delectable Mountains," Greatheart tells us. "Keep a look out for the shepherds. They'll be busy with their sheep, but we need to talk to them."

The shepherds see us first, and hurry down from the hills to say how pleased they are to find Greatheart. I can see why all the King's servants know and love him, for he's such a gentle and faithful guide – as well as a fearless killer of giants. The shepherds introduce themselves as Knowledge, Experience, Watchful and Sincere.

We talk until night, and the sky is clear, bright with stars. Despondency and his daughter Much-Afraid are tired and weak after their long imprisonment, so Greatheart asks the shepherds if they'll let us stay with them until tomorrow.

They welcome us to their tents, give us food and prepare beds for us. They say, "Come in, Mr. Feeble-Mind; come in, Mr. Ready-to-Halt; come in, Mr. Despondency and Much-Afraid."

The shepherd whose name is Watchful turns to Greatheart. "We're calling them by name," he explains, "because they're the ones who are most likely to hold back. The rest of you will come, I know. You are all welcome to stay with us."

That evening we have a hearty meal that will build us up for the journey ahead.

* * *

In the morning we wake refreshed and strengthened. The shepherds tell us they like to take their visitors up to see the view of the Celestial City, and many special places on the mountains, and ask if we would like to go.

Of course we all say yes, and enjoy our walk on the hills. I sit down at the top of the highest hill, staring into the distance. How different the view is from the one when my story starts, when I'm looking down on the City of Destruction.

In the distance, shining brightly among the distant hills, I'm sure I catch a glimpse the Celestial City. When everyone has seen the wonderful sights, Greatheart says there's still a little time to spare before we continue our journey. So instead of turning back to the tents, the shepherds offer to lead us to a hill called Mount Innocent where we see a man clothed all in white. Two men are throwing dirt at him.

"Stop them!" Mercy tells Greatheart. "They'll spoil his clothes."

"No," the shepherds say, "the King won't allow that."

Part 2 - Christiana's Story

As the man comes nearer, we can see that although the dirt is hitting his clothes, it doesn't leave the slightest mark.

"There must be a lesson in that," Mr. Honest says.

Watchful nods. "Those men are throwing dirt at the man in white because they hate the good way he lives. But, as you can see, the dirt won't stick to his clothes. It's like that with someone who lives truly for the King. Those men are wasting their time and energy for nothing. It's a good lesson for the King's pilgrims."

"And you only have yourselves to blame if the clothes the King gives become stained," Watchful adds. "None of your enemies has any power to spoil them."

We go to a hill called Mount Charity, where the shepherds show us a man with a roll of cloth. He's cutting coats and other clothes for the poor, but his roll of cloth never gets smaller.

"Why is this?" Samuel asks.

The shepherd called Sincere says, "Anyone who works to help those in need will never be in need themselves."

"When I was at the House Beautiful I read about a widow," I say. "The King made sure her pot of oil and sack of flour never ran out."

We stand silently for a long time, thinking back over the King's kindness to us since we started out as pilgrims. It seems such a long time ago that Goodwill, the King's Son, invited us in through the Wicket Gate.

Although the shepherds live in tents during the summer, Greatheart explains they also have a large house that the King has given as a place of rest for his pilgrims. When we return from our walk on the mountains, we find a meal prepared for us in the house. As soon as we've eaten it, Greatheart tells us to get ready for our journey, as he wants to set out in the early afternoon.

Mercy is standing with a sad look on her face. "I know it isn't right to keep wanting things, Christiana" she says quietly, "but I saw something just now that I would *so* like to have."

"What is it?" I ask.

"It's a small mirror in the dining room. I looked at it before the meal. On one side you can see yourself in it, but when you turn it round you don't see yourself, but the King's Son looking at you instead. Please ask the shepherds if they're willing to sell it."

I look at the mirror myself. It surely is one of a thousand. It shows me exactly as I am, but when I turn it round I can see the King's Son, just as Mercy said. There's the crown of thorns on his head, and he seems to smile at me. I realize that when I turn the mirror to look at *him*, I am no longer able to see myself. "The shepherds are kindhearted," I say. "Perhaps if they know you want it, they'll let you have it."

"I could buy it," Mercy says. "I have a little money."

"Well, don't cry anymore," I tell her. "I'll go and ask the shepherds about it."

The shepherds say, "Call her, call her. She shall certainly have what she wants."

I call Mercy, and Experience says, "Mercy, what is that thing you want?"

Mercy blushes. "The small mirror in the dining-room."

Part 2 - Christiana's Story

Sincere hurries and fetches it for her. Mercy bows her head and says, "Thank you, now I know that I have obtained favor in your eyes," which sounds a bit formal, but I know what she means.

The shepherds put a necklace on me, and another on Phoebe the daughter of Gaius, and also on Grace and Martha the daughters of Mnason. They then give us earrings, and a jewel for our foreheads. After wishing us a pleasant journey, the shepherds stand watching as we go down the road singing for joy.

CHAPTER 31
Valiant-for-Truth

Greatheart is leading the way, and he suddenly signals to us to stop. We are at the corner of a lane that leads from the Way of the King into the country of the evil prince. A man is standing with his sword in his hand, his face covered in blood.

Greatheart asks him what happened. The man is tall and strong, and I feel sure I've seen him before.

"My name is Valiant-for-Truth," the man says, "and I'm a pilgrim like yourselves. Three men came down this lane and attacked me. They told me I must take my choice of three things: to join them in robbing the King's pilgrims, to go back to my own City of Destruction, or be put to death on this spot."

"What did you say?" Greatheart asks.

"I told them I've always tried to be honest, and I certainly won't become a thief now. As for my own city, it was a bad place and I wouldn't have left it if I'd been happy living there. Then they asked me if I preferred to lose my life, and I said my life was worth too much for me to give it up lightly, and that they had no right to treat the King's servants like this. So they

Part 2 - Christiana's Story

drew their swords, and I drew mine, and we've been fighting for nearly three hours. They've wounded me, but I know I wounded them too. I suppose they must have heard you coming, for they suddenly turned and ran away."

"That was a hard battle, three men to one," Greatheart tells him, with a look of admiration on his face.

"Hard, yes," Valiant-for-Truth says, "but I knew I was fighting against my King's enemies, and that gave me courage."

Greatheart looks surprised. "Why didn't you cry for help? Some of the King's servants might have been near enough to hear you."

"I cried to the King himself, and I'm sure he answered me by sending you."

Greatheart smiles. "You're one of our King's true servants. Let me see your sword. Ah, yes, this is a Jerusalem blade, from the best armory."

"It's the best sword ever made," Valiant-for-Truth says. "No man who has so fine a weapon need be afraid, if he's learnt to use it skillfully."

Greatheart looks at Valiant-for-Truth in amazement. "You fought for three hours? Weren't you ready to drop with exhaustion?"

"No, as I fought, my sword clung to my hand and seemed to become part of my arm. I think that made me feel stronger."

"You've been courageous," Greatheart says. "You must finish your journey with us. We'll be glad of your company."

We make the soldier welcome. I wash his wounds, and Mercy and Phoebe help me bind them up. Grace and Martha get the boys to help them prepare some food, and tell Valiant-for-Truth he must rest for a while, for he has been in a bad fight. As the evening is coming on, we have to start once more on our journey.

I can see so many of us now, compared to the six of us who started out from the City of Destruction. There are my brothers: Matthew, Stephen, Joseph and James, and of course we were the first. Then along came Mercy, running after us before we reached the Wicket Gate. Next along the Way we picked up Phoebe the daughter of Gaius, then Martha and Grace at Mnason's house in Vanity Fair. Recently we found Feeble-Mind, Ready-to-Halt, Mr. Honest, Despondency and Much-Afraid. And now we have Valiant-for-Truth.

And of course, I mustn't forget Greatheart.

Part 2 - Christiana's Story

CHAPTER 32
Valiant-for-Truth's Son

I make sure I'm walking just behind Greatheart and Valiant-for-Truth, so I can hear everything the soldier says in answer to Greatheart's questions. He's telling Greatheart he once lived in the City of Destruction. I keep wondering where I've seen him before.

"What made you become a pilgrim?" Greatheart asks.

"I have a son," Valiant-for-Truth says. "When his mother, my wife, went to live with the King, he kept talking about the Celestial City. One morning started on a journey to find the King, and I was too busy to stop him and bring him back."

"What is your son's name?" Greatheart asks.

I listen impatiently for the answer, for now I feel sure I know who the soldier is.

"My son's name is Christian," the soldier says. "Someone called Truth told me how Christian fought with giants. Truth also said Christian was made welcome at all the King's lodgings, and when he came to the Gates of the Celestial City he was received with the sound of trumpets and a company of angels. Truth told how all the bells in the City rang for joy at Christian's reception, and what golden garments he was clothed with, with too many things to relate now. In a word, as Truth told the story, my heart told me to go after my son, for my work could not delay me any longer from finding the King. So here I am, on my way." He pauses and smiles broadly, in spite of the cuts on his arms and face from the fight.

Greatheart nods. "You came through the Wicket Gate then?"

"Indeed, yes," Valiant-for-Truth tells us all. "Truth told me that it would all be for nothing if I did not enter at the Gate."

"Do you remember me?" I ask shyly. I used to be rather in awe of Christian's father, for he always seemed too important to speak to someone like me.

"Why, yes," he says with a friendly wink. "You are Christian's friend, Christiana." He looks at the boys. "And these, I think, must be your four brothers. Well, I have to say how much you've all grown since I last saw you. It gladdens my heart to think that Christian will be greeting you, as well as looking out for me."

Greatheart and Valiant-for-Truth go on talking for some time, and the rest of us listen to Valiant-for-Truth's account of his pilgrimage. "My friends did everything they could to keep me in the City of Destruction," he says. "They told me that being a pilgrim was an idle life, and if I didn't want to be called lazy, I must never become one."

"Lazy?" I say in surprise, butting in. "It's been hard and dangerous work at times."

Part 2 - Christiana's Story

"But it's been good as well," James says. I wonder if he's only thinking about killing giants, but probably he also remembers the times in the King's houses along the Way.

"When that didn't work," Valiant-for-Truth continues, "my friends tried to frighten me by telling me about the dangers I'd meet if I became a pilgrim. They warned me of fierce giants, lions, Hill Difficulty and Apollyon the Destroyer. They told me I'll have to go over the Enchanted Ground, which is very dangerous."

"We're reaching that place soon," Greatheart says.

Valiant-for-Truth nods, but he doesn't seem worried. "They told me there's a place that's much worse than that," he continues. "They warned me of the Dark River, over which there is no bridge – and the River is between me and the Celestial City."

"Didn't all these things worry you?" Greatheart asks.

"No, they seemed but as so many nothings to me. I remembered what Truth said, and I knew he couldn't be deceiving me, so I left the city and began my journey. I even learnt a song to sing along the Way:

"Who would true valor see,
Let him come hither;
One here will constant be,
Come wind, come weather.
There's no discouragement
Shall make him once relent,
His first avowed intent
To be a pilgrim.

Chris Wright

> "Who so beset him round
> With dismal stories,
> Do but themselves confound.
> His strength the more is;
> No lion can him fright,
> He'll with a giant fight;
> But he will have a right
> To be a pilgrim.
>
> "Hobgoblin nor foul fiend
> Can daunt his spirit;
> He knows he at the end
> Shall life inherit.
> Then fancies fly away,
> He'll fear not what men say;
> He'll labor night and day
> To be a pilgrim."

It's not long before we all learn the words and join in. I play the viola and Mercy plays the lute as we walk along. It helps pass the time until we come to the Enchanted Ground.

Part 2 - Christiana's Story

CHAPTER 33
The Enchanted Ground

The Enchanted Ground is a strange place. As we enter it, we feel different. I begin to yawn and Greatheart is quick to notice.

"Be careful, everyone," he calls. "If any of you sit down to rest and fall asleep, you may never wake up again."

This frightens me so much that I feel wide awake – but only for a minute or two. I'm already starting to feel sleepy again.

Greatheart leads the way, for he's the guide, and Valiant-for-Truth follows at the back as the guard, in case some dragon or giant or thief attacks us from behind. Everyone who has a sword holds it tightly in their hands, for we know this is a dangerous place.

We cheer each other up as well as we can, but a great mist and darkness is hiding everything from sight. We can't even see each other, and keep calling out to be sure of staying together.

Greatheart and Valiant-For-Truth sound as though they're getting on well enough, but the rest of us are finding it painful. We keep huffing and puffing as we trip over a bush here, and get our shoes stuck in the soft ground there. James shouts that he's lost one of his shoes in the mud, but Matthew manages to get it back for him, even though he has to do it all by touch.

It's a great relief when the mist clears a little, and we see an arbor where we can rest. It's well built and covered with green branches, with seats inside. There's even a bed covered with springy moss..

"Make sure you all keep out of that shelter," Greatheart calls. "This resting place is called the Slothful's Friend, because it's been built by the evil prince to tempt pilgrims to stop, just when they feel they've had enough traveling."

I certainly feel like stopping for a bit, but of course I don't – not after that warning. It's completely dark as we press on, and Greatheart tells us to wait while he lights a lantern. "I need to be absolutely sure of what lies ahead of us," he says.

Greatheart holds the lamp up to read a map he's taken from his pocket. We all gasp when we see a pit right in the middle of our path.

"The King's enemies have dug this," Greatheart says. "It's full of water and mud. It may be extremely deep, and if you sink in there you could be lost forever."

Carefully, by the flickering light, we make our way around the muddy pit one at a time, trying not to look down into it. Feeble-Mind, Ready-to-Halt, Despondency and Much-Afraid need a lot of encouragement to keep going, but before long we are all safely back on the path.

We come to another arbor, and by Greatheart's light we see two men sleeping in it.

Part 2 - Christiana's Story

"These pilgrims have grown tired of their journey," Greatheart explains.

"Let's wake them up," Samuel says, and he hurries forward to shake the men by their shoulders.

"You're wasting your time," Greatheart tells him. "These two men have been sleeping here ever since I first passed this way."

Samuel shakes them hard, and one of the men mutters in his sleep, "I will fight so long as I can hold my sword in my hand."

Joseph and James laugh when they hear this, and I ask what it all means.

"It won't matter what we do," Greatheart explains. "We can shake them, shout at them and even hit them, and they'll always say something like that. They're probably dreaming they're still on their journey. I don't believe they will ever wake again, but their plight can be a warning to other pilgrims."

It's certainly a warning to me, and I want to keep going as fast as we can. Greatheart's lantern flickers out, leaving us in complete darkness. I begin to panic, and can hear Joseph and James crying. Greatheart calls to the King and strikes his light again. The lantern now burns brightly. A wind suddenly gets up and drives the last patches of mist away.

"Keep close," Greatheart warns. "We're not out of the Enchanted Ground yet."

I think I can hear someone talking, but the sound is too far in front to be sure. We come at last to a man on his knees, with his hands and eyes raised, talking solemnly to the King. He doesn't seem to know we're here, so we stand silently until he's finished.

He jumps up, and without looking round begins to hurry along the path in the direction of the Celestial City. Greatheart calls out, but the man only runs faster.

"I know you," Mr. Honest calls. "Your name is Mr. Stand-Fast. We used to live near each other. You're a good pilgrim."

Stand-Fast seems to recognize Mr. Honest's voice, and he turns and waits for us.

"Why were you running on like that?" Mr. Honest asks, with a hint of amusement in his voice.

"I have just met an evil witch," Stand-Fast says. "At first I thought she was a friend. She kept smiling at me, and showed me a purse full of money."

"I've heard of her," Mr. Honest says. "You are right, she is indeed a witch. She is the one who has causes pilgrims so much trouble on the Enchanted Ground. She represents everything in the world that causes us to forget about the King and his Son – riches, power, self-pleasing. These things are like a bubble that looks wonderful, but within an instant it becomes nothing. People often worship her and all she has to offer."

"I suspected as much," Stand-Fast says. "I called out to the King for help, and you came along at the right moment. I shudder to think what would have happened if I'd listened to her. I was finding the Enchanted Ground so difficult that I almost believed she was offering something easier and better than the Way of the King."

Mr. Honest nods. "You did well not to listen, or you would have been in great danger. Remember the old saying:
"Some, though they shun the frying pan,
Do leap into the fire!"

CHAPTER 34
Beulah

We're in the Land of Beulah now. The sun is shining, and Greatheart tells us it shines all day, but it never burns. I'm feeling tired after our journey, so I decide to lie down and rest in a house we've been given on the edge of an orchard.

Almost as soon as I get to sleep, the sound of bells on the other side of a wide river wakes me up. People are blowing trumpets, but I don't feel like complaining, for the music is so lovely.

I go to the window and see three angels walking along the road with a group of pilgrims. As they pass us, from the open window I can hear the angels saying words of comfort to the pilgrims who look so weary.

My ears are now filled with such beautiful sounds that I know I've never felt so at peace before. I can almost imagine I'm in the Celestial City, even though it's on the other side of what people are calling the Dark River.

I go out into the orchard, and some children run up to me with bunches of flowers. They have enough for Mercy, and yet

Part 2 - Christiana's Story

more for Phoebe, Grace and Martha. My four brothers are sitting together, talking under an apple tree – and I doubt if they want flowers.

I think perhaps Matthew will make a good teacher, as he's become so wise lately. He smiles when I go across and tell him this.

"I'd like to be a teacher, if the King chooses the work for me," he says.

I tell Samuel he'll make a good soldier like Greatheart.

"To guide the pilgrims?" he asks. "Yes," he says thoughtfully, "that would be the best work of all. But I can never be as good at it as Greatheart."

I laugh. "Do you think Greatheart was always good? He must have been trained, or he wouldn't know so much about the King and his ways. You're brave and careful. You'll make a good guide."

Joseph and James tell me they've done enough traveling for now, but I can see the journey has done them good. I wonder what the King has in mind for them.

Mercy joins us now. "We were so few when we started," she says as she sits down on the grass. "Now look how many of us there are here in Beulah. Some young and some old, some weak and some strong, and yet the King has cared for us all."

I see Matthew looking at her with a smile on his face, and I remember the words of Gaius. Yes, maybe they will marry one day, and serve the King together.

CHAPTER 35
The Message

It is now many years later. Matthew has indeed married my best friend Mercy, and together they are teaching young pilgrims, along with three children of their own. More of a surprise was the marriage of Samuel to Grace, the daughter of Mnason. They have a baby boy. Joseph is engaged to Grace's sister Martha. Phoebe, the daughter of Gaius, always seems to be with James. Meeting young Phoebe at the inn of Gaius seems like a distant memory now.

I'm pleased to know that my brothers are with true followers of the King.

Mr. Honest, and many of the other pilgrims we journeyed with, have already crossed the Dark River, and are now at peace in the Celestial City. Before leaving us, Stand-Fast said, "I am going to see that Head that was crowned with thorns." We all knew he was referring to the King's Son, for it is a story we love to tell each other.

Christian's father, Valiant-for-Truth, crossed over a few months ago. He said he was proud to have received so many

Part 2 - Christiana's Story

cuts and injuries for the King. He gave his sword to Samuel who is training to be one of the King's soldiers and guides, just like Greatheart. So finally Valiant-for-Truth is with his wife and with his son Christian.

I know I'll be there myself soon, but I'm not sad or anxious. Sometimes the water is high and rough, but I know the King's Son will be on the other side to welcome me.

An angel came yesterday with a message for Ready-to-Halt. He crossed the Dark River last night, and I can picture him now, healed and running and dancing for joy in the Celestial City. When he came to the edge of the Dark River, he said, "Now I shall have no more need of these crutches, because on the other side are chariots and horses for me to ride on!"

Before going, he asked for his crutches to be given to another pilgrim in need of support, "With a hundred warm wishes that he may travel better than I have done."

I keep thinking back to the time when I sat on the hill above the City of Destruction. How different life was for me then. I knew nothing of the love of the King and his Son, and I knew nothing of the joy that is waiting for me now in the Celestial City. I hear a knock at the door. I open it and an angel stands there with a message from the King.

"Greetings, Christiana," the angel says. "I bring you news that the King is calling you, and wants you to stand in his presence, in clothes of everlasting life."

"I'm coming, Lord," I say, "to be with you and bless you for ever."

THE END

NOTE

Well, that really is the end, but you can find more about the meaning behind this story by going to the *Young Pilgrim's Progress* link on the Lighthouse Christian Publishing website:
www.lighthousechristianpublishing.com

* * *

Chris Wright is the author of over thirty books, starting with young fiction for an English Christian publisher in 1966. He has written both fiction and non-fiction, mostly with a Christian theme, for a variety of publishers. Chris is married with three grownup children, and lives in the West Country of England where he is a home group leader with his local church. His personal website is: www.rocky-island.com

1111406

Made in the USA